TALES FROM A SHATTERED WORLD

A SHORT STORY COLLECTION

J.A. ROGGIE

GRINNING BARD PRESS LLC.

Also by

J.A. Roggie

<u>Novels</u>
The Book of Devaultus
<u>Short Fiction</u>
Devaultus Was Here

CONTENTS

ONE

FLOWERS FOR MARIBEL

Delph stood at the edge of the overgrown path, staring up at the wall of trees that loomed ahead like ancient sentinels. Their trunks were thick and gnarled, bark furrowed like old skin, each one soaked in the deep browns and soft greens of a forest that had seen too many seasons to care about men. The leaves above rustled gently in the wind, whispering secrets to one another. A damp, earthy scent rose from the soil, rich with decay and life, like the breath of the world itself. Somewhere in the distance, a bird called out, a lonely, high-pitched trill that echoed through the underbrush and faded into silence.

He sighed, the sound catching in his throat like an old memory, and turned to glance back at the trailer behind him. It sagged under its own weight, the paint peeling, porch steps crooked and falling apart. A rusty swing swayed in the breeze, squeaking with each movement.

Ninety-four years old. That was how long he had lived on this planet, and most folks didn't think a man his age should be wandering around at all, let alone in the woods by himself. Hell, most didn't think he should be doing anything by himself anymore. They whispered things about safety and fall risks and caretakers. They said it like he was already gone.

His chest tightened, not from the walk, but from the ache that never quite left. His wife, God bless her sweet soul, had passed three years ago. And when she left, it felt like the color drained out of the world. Without both their checks coming in, and with the burial cost, he lost their condo. The military checks helped, but not enough. Nothing ever seemed to be enough anymore.

So, they shipped him here. Out of the city, to the middle of nowhere. To live with his grandson.

He turned back toward the trailer again; eyes narrowed beneath his heavy brows. He loved the boy. That much hadn't changed. The drugs had sunk their claws deep in the boy, leaving him a ghost of the bright kid he used to be. Right now, he was probably passed out in his room, strung out on something so twisted and unnatural that God Himself would have wept to see it.

Delph's checks from the military had quietly been disappearing for months now. He had an idea where they were going.

Delph, or rather, Sergeant Delph Marisson, retired, scratched his balding head as he turned back toward the looming wall of trees. Somewhere in that dense green was Lulu, his late wife's cat. The little devil had slipped out while he was fumbling for the morning paper, vanishing into the brush like a whisper on the wind.

Lulu was a menace. Pure trouble wrapped in gray fur, but he loved her. Would never say it out loud, mind you. It wasn't proper for a man like him, not becoming of a sergeant to go around getting mushy over a cat. But Lulu had been Maribel's. The last living piece of her in this world, and that meant something.

To be fair, even the memories of Maribel were slipping these days. Some mornings he woke up certain she'd just stepped out of the room, and other days he couldn't recall the exact color of her eyes. That tore at him more than anything else.

He let out a rough grunt and rolled his shoulders. "Well, Lulu," he muttered, "I guess if I'm going to find you, I'd better get moving."

His eyes drifted back to the wall of trees. Thick trunks pressed tight together; branches knotted overhead like old bones. It looked like a place that didn't want visitors. But just as he was about to give up and hope Lulu returned on her own, his gaze landed on a narrow gap in the underbrush. A break, just barely wide enough for an old man to squeeze through.

With a grunt, he shuffled forward. His knees creaked in protest as he crouched, the joints popping like snapping twigs. Damp leaves brushed his arms, and the cool scent of moss curled into his nose. The air here was different, cleaner.

He pushed his way through the opening and stumbled into a clearing on the other side.

"Lulu?" he called, his voice soft and gravelly. It didn't carry far.

Only silence answered him.

He turned, glancing back toward the narrow break in the wall of trees, trying to mark its location in his mind. The opening was already starting to blend into the green behind him, as if the forest was trying to swallow it whole. Slowly, deliberately, Delph began to take in his surroundings.

What stretched out before him was a place untouched by human hands for what felt like centuries. Not even the faintest echo of civilization lingered. Just a few feet beyond the homes of addicts and desperation, this place bloomed like a secret Eden, beautiful, quiet, and pure. The air smelled sweet with wildflowers and rich fragrance. Birds chirped softly in the canopy above, and somewhere nearby, the wings of insects hummed like tiny violins.

To his right lay a wide pond, its glassy surface rippling beneath the golden sunlight. Delph squinted and smiled as he spotted lazy dorsal fins slicing through the water, the fish basking in the warmth, just beneath the surface. It was the kind of peace that made you forget the rest of the world existed.

A deep, contented smile spread across his weathered face.

He remembered his own grandfather then, how they used to sit on a muddy riverbank with old fishing poles and a coffee can full of worms. Delph had been a terrible fisherman. Couldn't catch a cold if he fell in. But his grandfather? That man could yank a bass out of a mud puddle with a bent nail and string. He chuckled softly, eyes still on the pond.

If he were here, he'd already be seated, line in the water and sun on his face, grinning like everything was right in the world.

"I'll have to come back here," Delph murmured, mostly to himself. "Bring a pole, maybe a sandwich. Just sit and listen to the water for a while."

He turned, heart a little lighter than it had been in weeks, and that was when he saw her. Lulu. The gray streak of fur danced up a winding path that twisted through the trees like it had been carved by wind and time. It led upward, toward another clearing bathed in soft, dappled light.

"Lulu? Come here, girl," he called gently.

But Lulu had her own ideas. She never even looked back, just padded gracefully up the path, tail flicking in the air tauntingly.

Delph sighed and continued after her, boots crunching softly on the forest path. Halfway up the hill, he paused and glanced back at the pond below. For a moment, he thought he saw someone sitting on the bank with a fishing pole in hand. The figure was still, relaxed, just like his grandfather used to be. A crooked smile tugged at Delph's lips. He lifted his hand in a slow wave, feeling a flicker of warmth in his chest.

It looked so much like him.

But as quickly as the vision appeared, it faded, like smoke dissolving in the wind. The figure was gone, and the bank sat empty again. His smile dimmed. His old mind liked to play these tricks, dragging up memories when he least expected them. It didn't worry him anymore; it was just part of the way things worked now. Still, it hurt when the face of someone you loved slipped away like that, piece by piece.

He turned back to the trail and climbed.

On the next rise, the forest opened into a wide ledge bathed in radiant sunlight. Lulu was there, prancing in the grass and chasing a butterfly with the enthusiasm of a kitten. Delph chuckled, the sound gravelly but warm. She wasn't a young cat anymore, but she moved with a spring in her step that defied the years.

"I wish I had half your energy," he muttered with a wheeze as he leaned on his knees.

The clearing around him was beautiful, soft moss underfoot, wildflowers swaying in a light breeze that carried the scent of pine and something sweet he couldn't quite place. He crouched down slowly, his knees protesting the motion, and picked a pair of small white flowers. He used to do that for Maribel when they were young, back when wildflowers and laughter were all they needed to get through the day.

"Maybe I'll give these to you when I get back," he whispered, holding them gently between weathered fingers. For a moment forgetting his love was gone.

He rose and continued onward, the forest swaying around him as he climbed. The trail led to a vast open plateau ringed by trees so tall their tops were lost in the light above. To his left, a group of wild horses grazed peacefully in the tall grass. They lifted their heads at his approach, dark eyes studying him with quiet intelligence.

They didn't bolt. They didn't panic.

They simply watched him, like they understood something he didn't yet know.

Delph stood there, watching the wild horses as they grazed peacefully before him. The soft breeze stirred their manes, making the scene feel almost dreamlike. His eyes followed a young buckskin filly, bouncing and prancing in the field with carefree joy. She seemed to have no worries at all, moving with a freedom that Delph hadn't felt in years.

He smiled quietly to himself, content just to observe. It had been many years since he'd seen anything so pure, so untouched. These animals were at peace with the world around them, and in that moment, Delph felt the weight of the world, his aches, grief, and struggles of his days, slip away.

He watched them for what must have been close to half an hour, his heart lightened by their antics, their grace. He couldn't help but laugh softly as the young filly kicked up her hooves, spinning in circles as if the very ground beneath her feet was a dance floor. The world here was different, simpler. And for the first time in a long while, Delph felt like everything was well in the world.

But then, with a slight shake of his head, he remembered his purpose. Lulu. Where had she gone? His eyes scanned the field, searching for the familiar grey streak of her fur.

His gaze shifted, and there before him, was something even more stunning than the horses. The entire area seemed enclosed, protected by a towering cliff face that arched around him, guarding the peaceful land from the harshness of the outside world. It was like nature itself had built a sanctuary here, keeping all the worries and troubles of the world at bay.

Delph took a step forward, his old knees creaking slightly. As he did, his eyes were drawn to the water cascading gracefully from the cliff face. The waterfall fell in a soft, steady rhythm, pooling into a crystal-clear pond below, its surface gleaming in the sunlight like polished glass.

"How beautiful..." Delph whispered, a quiet, wistful smile tugging at his lips. "Maribel would have loved this."

He slowly crouched down, reaching out toward the water, his fingers brushing against the smooth stones lining the edge. The water was so clear, so pristine. Beneath the surface, small lizards darted playfully, their lithe bodies weaving between the rocks.

Delph chuckled softly, the sound carrying the weight of a thousand memories. He remembered how, as a boy, he and his sister would catch little creatures like these, before the world had gotten so complicated, before screens and devices stole their attention.

He dipped his hand into the water, letting the coolness of it seep into his weathered skin. He waited patiently as the lizards swam closer. It wasn't long before one glided over his palm, its tiny feet brushing against him. Without a second thought, Delph closed his hand, catching the little creature in his grasp.

For a moment, he held it there, the soft thrum of its tiny body against his palm, feeling an unexpected connection to the wildness around him. The peacefulness, the simplicity, the sheer beauty of the world he had stumbled upon was almost too much to grasp. But for once, Delph didn't mind. He let the moment overtake him, just for a breath.

Delph gently lifted one of the little newts from the water, his heart lightening at the sight of its tiny, delicate form. A smile spread across his face, soft and full of warmth. "Hello, little fella," he murmured, the joy of the moment blooming in his chest. There was something comforting about holding life, even this small, simple creature. Slowly, he lowered his hand, allowing the newt to swim free again. As it disappeared beneath the surface, a single tear slipped down Delph's cheek. Joy brought on by his memories overtaking him.

He wiped his cheek with the back of his hand and, with a sigh, rose to his feet, his joints creaking slightly in protest. He stood for a moment, taking in the quiet beauty around him, then continued his journey through the clearing, his old legs carrying him forward with steady, deliberate steps.

But then, his eyes fell upon something that stopped him in his tracks. A house nestled just below the towering stone cliff face. Water tumbled over the edge of the cliff, creating another waterfall that cascaded down, forming a small stream that wound its way around the house. The house itself was untouched, pristine, and it seemed to shimmer in the soft light. It was a place that had been cared for, loved even, but it seemed as though it had been forgotten by time.

Delph's breath caught in his chest as he slowly made his way toward the house, drawn to it as if something inside was calling him. The stream babbled gently as he crossed a small wooden bridge that arched over it. He made his way up the stairs, each step bringing him closer to the strange, peaceful world he had stumbled upon.

Reaching the door, Delph hesitated for a moment before knocking softly. Of course, there was no one here, how could there be? A place like this, so far removed from everything. But then, as if to answer his doubt, a voice came from within.

"Come in!" The voice was soft and welcoming, a woman's voice, clear, melodic, and strangely familiar.

Delph's hand trembled as he reached up to turn the doorknob. With a slow breath, he stepped inside. At first, the bright light of the room blinded him, but as his eyes adjusted, he found himself standing in a cozy dining room. And there, at the table, sat a woman: his wife, Maribel.

Her soft laughter filled the air as she sat with Lulu curled up in her lap, exactly as Delph remembered her, the way she had looked when they first met, so full of life and warmth.

"Mar? Is... Is that you?" His voice cracked, the weight of the years falling away as he spoke her name.

She giggled, that sweet, sing-song voice he had loved so much. "It's me, Del. Come in. Get yourself something to eat."

Delph took a few hesitant steps forward, the room spinning slightly around him. His eyes were drawn to a full-length mirror on the far wall, and as he gazed into it, he froze, his breath catching in his chest.

There, reflected in the glass, was his younger self, twenty-two again. He was strong, well-muscled from years of hard work. He looked so... whole. So alive. He felt no pain or trembling; his weariness was gone.

He blinked, his heart racing as he turned back to her, his voice cracked. "Mar?" he whispered again, unable to understand what his eyes were telling him.

She smiled at him, her eyes shining with warmth that made Delph's heart ache. "It's different here," she said softly, her voice like a soothing melody. "You, we... we're young and vibrant. We can stay here forever together. Just you and me."

Delph's chest tightened, and before he could stop it, tears welled up in his eyes. They spilled over, tracing a slow path down his weathered face. He couldn't help it, the weight of years, pain of loss, the longing for this impossible dream, it all broke through. He stepped forward, his hands trembling as he held out the delicate flowers he had picked earlier.

He half-expected them to vanish in his hands like so many other illusions, like the memories that had slipped from his mind over time. He braced himself for the sting of disappointment. But instead, she reached out, her fingers soft as she took the flowers from him. She lifted them to her nose, inhaling their sweet scent deeply, a small smile curling at the corners of her lips.

Delph's heart swelled at the sight. A gentle warmth spread through him, peace, like a balm to the ache in his soul. He watched her for a moment, his tears falling freely now, each drop a mixture of joy and sorrow. This was real. *She* was real, standing in front of him.

Maribel looked up at him, her eyes locking with his, and for the first time in a long while, Delph felt a genuine warmth fill his heart. Slowly, he seated himself at the table, the chair creaking beneath him. The weight of years of grief seemed to lift, if only for a moment. Here, in this strange, beautiful place, he was with her again.

Two

Better Luck Next Time

I am Conner Artorious.

Number one best explorer of all time. Ever. Period. Not that it means much these days, explorers are a dying breed. Metaphorically, sure. But also, literally. Let me explain.

I was born on a small, half-forgotten planet called Earth. The year is 2073, and we've done what humanity does best: ruined a perfectly good thing. We turned paradise into ash. Torched our own home and then acted surprised when the fire burned us too.

Earth is now a wasteland. Cracked dirt, and poisoned skies. You know the kind of place where hope goes to die with a whimper and a cough. The last estimate put our population at around three hundred thousand souls. Give or take a few thousand. Hard to keep a headcount when most comms are fried and half the people left don't want to be found.

In the mood for some water? Well, too bad, that's a luxury. What about some good food? Scratch that, what about any food? How unfortunate because that's just a memory. We scrape by on scraps and synth-paste, and even that's starting to run low.

And that...well, that's where I come in.

Our communities have been working together on something strange. Desperate, yes, but odd in a way that just might save us. We're trying to pull water from things that shouldn't give water at all. Let me explain.

Everything in the world contains water on some level. Even the driest objects, like rocks, dust or rusted-out machinery, hold trace amounts deep down at the molecular level. Water is everywhere. Just not in such a way that we can drink it.

Now, the few scientists we have left, and I use the word "scientists" loosely as most of them were chem teachers or amateur physicists before everything collapsed. I mean we even have some guy named Jim who did none of those. All he did was tell them, "I once had a science kit when I was five." So, they gave him a lab coat and *bam*, suddenly he's a scientist. Okay, they have a theory. I'm not saying it's a bad one. Let me tell you what it is.

They believe we can extract water using a process called Acoustic Levitation. It's an old concept, something that used to be more sci-fi than science. Basically, they use sound waves to manipulate matter. Turn the right frequency loose on the right material and, in theory, you can separate molecules. That includes pulling water out of solid objects.

It sounds insane. But then again, surviving in a dead world is insane already. If this works, even partially, it could buy us time. Maybe a few more years, or perhaps just long enough to find another way to keep breathing.

Anyways, there were these three scientists and of course, Jim. No idea why they always ask Jim, but together they cobbled together this acoustic levitation device and stuck it in the gymnasium of the old school.

They all worked hard to get it functional. After weeks of scavenging parts and tuning frequencies, the thing finally powered up. It started vibrating, humming, doing its sonic thing. Looked like it might actually work.

But they missed something.

They didn't properly account for the speed at which it would vibrate. Someone botched the math. Yeah, you guessed it. It was Jim. The levitation unit didn't just float particles or shift air, it bent reality. Everything around them wobbled, like the fabric of space itself had a hiccup.

Jim, being a guy who always seems to get himself in far over his head, was naturally standing right next to it when the whole thing went sideways. He began to shake. Not a normal kind of shake, but an oh-no-the-universe-is-melting kind of shake.

And here's where things got... complicated.

According to String Theory, reality isn't just one flat pancake of existence. There are multiple dimensions layered on top of ours. Folded, twisted, compactified realms, and yes *compactified* is the scientific term... I think. Anyway, each vibrating at its own unique frequency.

Well, someone, I can't say who, screamed that the machine had hit the natural vibrational frequency of one of those hidden dimensions.

And *boom*.

A micro-wormhole tore open, and just like that, one moment, they were in a busted-up gym. The next, someone got yanked into a tear in space. Jim was the one who got pulled in like a little girl holding the leash of a mastiff.

Now, he's sitting in a weird jungle. The plants don't look right, the air hums with electricity, and the birds have way too many eyes. This place evolved differently. Completely.

Which brings us to the awkward part.

Yeah... Jim's not here. He never was.

In fact: There *is* no Jim.

I didn't plan to be an explorer, alright? That was never the goal. But I'm the one who got pulled through the wormhole. And this whole time, this whole story, the "Jim" you've been hearing about?

That's me.

I've been Jim. I just didn't want to admit it until now.

You happy?

This isn't what I signed up for. Not by a long shot. I didn't ask to be yanked into some alternate dimension jungle where even the fruit comes with a disclaimer.

Granted, I will say this. I did manage to find something that *might* pass for edible. See, after hours of stumbling through oversized ferns and dodging vines that looked like they wanted to shake hands, I spotted one of the strange birds of this world.

These weren't Earth birds. Picture a parrot, then stretch its neck like a periscope, paint it a flat black with stripes of glowing teal, and give it a set of wings that hum instead of flap, kind of like some kind of crazy hummingbird. Also, it had four legs. Like it couldn't decide between being a bird or a cat and went with "Yes."

Anyway, it hopped right up to a low-hanging fruit, shaped like a cluster of jiggly grey grapes. The strange fruits were fused into a sort of jelly orb that wobbled at the slightest breeze. The bird gave it a few pecks, chirped something that sounded like a kazoo being strangled, and started eating. There was no death, spasms, or imploding. It finished its snack and zipped away, happy as a freaky little clam.

So, I marked that fruit down as "probably safe."

Then I saw the *other* fruit.

This one was about the size of a softball, deep purple with pulsing green veins and little thorny ridges around its base. It looked juicy, almost tempting. Until another of those alien birds landed nearby and gave it a nibble.

Well, that was a big mistake.

The moment its beak touched the skin, the fruit split open like a trap. It clamped onto the bird's face with rows of thorny teeth and started secreting this milky, acidic goo. The poor thing squawked, flailed, and then collapsed. The fruit just... absorbed it. Sucked the bird in and sealed back up like it had never opened in the first place.

Needless to say, that one is on my do-not-eat list.

So here I am, sitting in this weird borderline psycho jungle with a handful of mystery grapes that haven't tried to eat me yet. It's not much, but it's a start. Welcome to survival, alternate dimension edition.

Overall, in comparison to Earth Prime...at least, that's what I'm going to call it. Yeah, I know. Sounds a little megalomaniac to assume that every alternate dimension Earth starts from mine, but it's my story, Thank you very much. So, it's Earth Prime and my Earth is the starting pancake. Who's going to argue with me? The jungle?

Didn't think so.

Now, surviving in this place? That's a whole other mess entirely. I've been trekking through this overgrown nightmare with nothing but instinct, and a few scraps of common sense.

The first creature I ran into looked like a gorilla stapled to a centipede. It had twelve legs, glowing red eyes, and a temper that made it allergic to pretty much anything breathing. I only got away because it was too big to fit between two massive tree trunks and got stuck long enough for me to slip past. I looked back and saw its backside wriggling helplessly, wedged between the trunks as it tried to free itself. Reminded me a bit of my ex, Margot. I won't deny I laughed. I'm sorry, Margot. Well, sort of.

Another time, I stumbled into a clearing filled with what I thought were giant flowers. Beautiful, glowing, swaying gently in the wind. I moved closer, thinking maybe, just maybe, I could catch some rest in the soft grass beneath them.

Turns out, they weren't flowers. They were mouths. With tentacle-petal tongues. They snapped shut the moment I stepped near. Missed me by inches. One actually tried to *crawl* after me. Yes, crawl. Like a hungry daisy with abandonment issues.

Eventually, I got smarter. I watched the local wildlife, followed the smaller creatures that weren't actively being eaten. Some of them resembled rabbits, if rabbits were made of glassy chitin and could camouflage themselves by blending into the moss. I started tracking them, learned which plants they nibbled, and gave those a shot.

I found a kind of blue-stemmed fern with leaves that tasted like licorice and didn't try to strangle me afterward. Jackpot. I also managed to catch one of those rabbit-bug hybrids using a makeshift snare. Roasted it over a fire made from dried vine husks and slammed a few rocks together to make a spark. Definitely harder than the books make it seem. It smelled like burnt tires but tasted halfway decent.

So here I am, still alive, un-eaten, and Earth Prime's least-qualified explorer making his mark in a world.

Finally, I found the perfect spot. A clearing right next to a stream. Flowing water, room to move, and, at least as far as I could tell, without a topographic map or any knowledge of the weather patterns, outside of a flood zone. That's as scientific as I can get without my old lab coat, which I'll remind you does not help you be more of a scientist.

It took some time, but I found a stone that could be chipped into something resembling a knife. And by "knife," I mean a glorified rock shard that doesn't seem to be able to cut butter. I wish I could tell you I was smart enough to carry one with me but come on, do I look like the type of guy who is on a television show eating bugs? I'm the kind of guy who once owned a science kit, got really good at baking soda volcanoes, and somehow stumbled his way into being one of the leading scientists left on Earth. So no, I didn't bring a knife. Don't judge me. I'm trying.

Anyway, with my totally-not-useless blade in hand, I started the slow, soul-sucking process of cutting down tree limbs to make a shelter. With something as sharp as a plastic spork, I'll remind you. It was well into the night by the time I finished, which... yeah, not my finest hour. You'd think someone with my credentials could handle basic survival stuff with style and grace. Turns out, I can't.

The shelter I built? It's awful. Honestly, a strong breeze could bring it down. Thankfully strong breezes don't seem to happen often here. But it's standing, kinda. Okay, listen, it counts.

Here's the thing that keeps tugging at me though. I haven't seen any signs of other humans. No footprints, no half-burned campfires, not even a broken Coke bottle. Nothing. Am I the only one here?

Because if I am... well, this might be the start of something new. A fresh world, untouched by human hands. A blank canvas, a perfect paradise. You know, in case we want to ruin it all over again.

At this point, I'd been here a couple of days. Long enough to evolve my sad little shelter from "third-world shack" to "Hey, look, Ma, I built a fort!" I was proud, okay? It had four walls. Well, three and a leaning one, and it only leaked in *most* places. Progress.

Of course, I'm still pretty sure a centi-rilla could knock it over; yeah, that's a centipede and a gorilla had a horrifying lovechild, you know, Margot? Yup, okay, good we're back on track. That thing could knock it flat with one annoyed backhand. But hey, let's just collectively hope it doesn't come to that. Please.

I finally sat down to clear my head and make a game plan. I needed direction. Focus. A mission. I needed a little piece of Earth Prime to keep me grounded, even if Earth Prime had kicked me through a dimensional wormhole and left me dead.

So, I started to plan.

Not just *plan*, mind you, but build. I began drawing up where the different buildings would go. A lab over here, maybe a hydroponic farm near the stream, some housing pods up the ridge, and of course, a spot for the coffee bar. Priorities.

I even began to build. Little foundations, markers, frames made from bent branches and vines. Nothing crazy, but enough to feel real. I told myself it was preparation. For their arrival, you know when *they* got here.

Who's "they"? I don't know. The rescue team? Maybe future settlers? My imaginary science friends who live in my head now?

Either way, I wasn't just surviving anymore. I was preparing for civilization. Or madness. Possibly both.

It's been twenty years.

Two whole decades in this place. No one ever came to find me. And, somewhere around six months in, right about the time I tried to make coffee out of moss, I realized the truth: the math that brought me here? It was mine.

My equations, calculations, and cosmic screw-up. It was all mine. I had scribbled the numbers that cracked reality on my arm, which was obviously with me now and no one else knew how I came up with them. It would take them a miracle to recreate it. And Earth Prime was a bit short on miracles these days.

So here I am, stuck alone, in paradise.

That's the real twist. This world? It's not some hellscape. No sulfur pits or screaming skies. Just... beauty. Endless jungle, clean water, bizarre fruit that only sometimes tries to eat you if you pick the wrong ones. It's perfect.

Perfectly empty.

I assume the worst. Maybe Earth Prime is gone. Wiped out. Or perhaps the experiment blew the whole planet to bits and I'm the only leftover flake drifting in the cosmic wind. Last man standing in a world not meant for men.

And you know what? Maybe that's for the best.

I've told myself that over the years. Said it out loud. Wrote it down even, on tree bark. Hundreds of entries. Journals carved into nature like a madman's manifesto. Not that anyone's going to read it. Not unless some future alien archaeologist shows up and decides my ramblings are sacred text.

I went full *Cast Away,* by the way. Yeah, that stage hit me hard. I found a beetle, he was a big sucker, had on him a shiny shell and looked like he knew things. I named him Jim. Don't judge me, it was all I could think of. I talked to him every day.

He got yelled at when the roof collapsed. I blamed him when the traps didn't catch anything. That time when I got sick off that one mushroom? Blamed him for that too.

I hate you, Jim.

But then again... Jim's the reason I'm here, isn't he?

I laughed at myself.

It came out rough. Hollow... dry, like my laugh was a ball I threw without anyone around to catch it.

The memory hit me like a book cover to the face. "The Silent Towns." I must've read it a hundred times growing up. That story always stuck with me. A man alone, thinking he's the last, until a crazy woman shows up and makes him wish he was. At this point? I think I'd take it. Crazy and all. Hell, I'd even take someone who talked too much about cats. Maybe.

But there's no one coming, not anymore.

Jim's long gone now. Yeah, Jim, The Beetle, you know my emotional support therapy-bug. My scapegoat. My only companion. One night, some odd snake-otter-like thing slipped through the gaps in the outer wall. Nasty little hybrid. Cute, if you ignored the extra eyelids and the whole "eats your friends" thing. Took Jim in one gulp. He didn't even have the courtesy to burp. Just slithered off like it hadn't devoured my last tether to sanity.

Now it's just me.

I sit on the porch of my house, if you could call it that. Took me ten years to get it this good. Bamboo, mudstone, vines twisted just right. Not bad for a scientist who once set his own microwave on fire reheating spaghetti.

My feet are kicked up. The breeze smells like citrus and cinnamon. I'm sipping tea I make from these purple leaves that only bloom after it rains, mixed with some sweet melon-fruit that drips sap like syrup. Tastes like those strange cool-aid packs, and strangely mustard. I know, it's an odd combination. But after a while you get less picky.

I lift the cup to the sky. No stars yet. Just the slow swirl of color this planet does when it starts to sleep.

"Here's to humankind," I say aloud. Just in case the sky's listening. "When you write about me. Just remember. I didn't sign up for this."

I raise the cup a little higher.

"Better luck next time."

And I drink.

Three

Keep the Change

A soft *blurp* echoed from the water dispenser, the sound oddly loud in the quiet hum of fluorescent lights. Lukewarm water splashed into a paper cup, trembling slightly in Bill's hand.

"That can't be true," said one of the two men loitering near the cooler, his voice low and incredulous.

"No, seriously. I was there. I *saw* it."

Bill, stocky, sweat-prone, and visibly losing the war with his receding hairline, shifted his weight, the buttons of his ill-fitting shirt threatening mutiny across his gut. His beard, thick and disheveled, looked like it had last seen a comb during the Bush administration.

Across from him stood Edgar, tall and rail-thin, like a coat rack that had somehow learned how to gossip. His eyes were ringed with dark circles deep enough to store secrets, and a subtle twitch jerked at the corner of his mouth every few seconds. The man reeked of sleep deprivation and off-brand energy drinks.

"You're telling me," Bill said slowly, "that you saw *Jessica*... at *Pinky's Bar*... with *the boss*?"

Edgar nodded solemnly, eyes wide. "They were *all over each other*, man. Like full-on PDA. Tongues. Hands. The works."

Bill squinted at him, trying to decide what was harder to believe: Edgar actually setting foot in a bar, or Jessica, office bombshell and fashion risk enthusiast, getting cozy with Marty, the balding middle manager with anger management issues.

But before he could say anything, a thought struck him. He frowned.

"Hold up, Edgar. So... he's cheating on his wife?"

Edgar shook his head. "Nah, man. His wife *disappeared* like six months ago. Just packed up and ghosted. She owed him some money or something, and boom, gone."

Bill blinked. "Wow. So, she was like, 'Nope,' and just vanished with his cash?"

"That's what I heard," Edgar said with a shrug.

"He's been telling everyone he lost his wife. It's really working to get that sympathy lay."

Bill looked at him wide-eyed. "Huh, so that works, huh?" he asked.

Edgar nodded. "Based off the noises coming from Marty's office when he thinks everyone is on lunch. I'd say it does."

"So, I'd say he's... kinda a free agent right now," Edgar said with a smirk.

Bill nodded slowly. "Yeah... *kinda.*"

Jessica, with her scandalously short skirts and shirts that looked to be fighting entirely too hard to keep her contained, wasn't exactly shy about her assets. But *still*. The *boss*? *Pinky's*?

"Well, I'll be damned," Bill muttered, taking a sip from his water cup like it was whiskey and not budget-brand hydration. He stared blankly into the middle distance, his brain doing the slow, painful math of what this meant for Monday's team meeting.

Edgar stared off into the same awkward middle distance as Bill, both of them chewing on silence like stale gum.

"Yup," Edgar finally said.

"Yup," Bill echoed, just as solemn.

A blur of motion broke the stillness; some kid darted past, nearly knocking over a stack of printer paper. Bill rolled his eyes so hard, it was a miracle they didn't get stuck.

"I still can't believe Marty let Janice bring her kid to work," he grumbled. "How the hell are we supposed to get anything done with that little goblin running around like it's recess?"

Edgar gave a slow nod of agreement. "I *know*, man. This ain't bring-your-kid-to-work day, it's bring-your-anxiety-to-a-boil day. But let's face it... Marty's got his hands full these days. Y'know, with *Jessica* and all."

He chuckled, but the laugh quickly dissolved into a ragged cough that rattled deep in his chest. It didn't stop. It just *kept going*, long enough for it to become uncomfortable.

Bill watched him with concern, one eyebrow creeping up. "You gonna make it, man?"

Edgar held up a finger as if asking for divine patience, then finally wiped sweat from his brow. "Yeah. Yeah, I'm good," he said, breathless.

Bill took a sip from his paper cup, eyes narrowing. "You really need to quit smoking. It's gonna kill you."

Edgar gave a dry laugh that turned bitter at the edges. "Keep working here and I'll beat it to the punch."

Bill snorted, raising his cup in mock salute. "That's fair, I guess."

The sudden *click-clack* of high heels on linoleum snapped their attention to the corner. And of course, it was *her*.

Jessica strutted into view like she owned the damn building. She didn't so much walk as glide, hips swaying, hair bouncing as much as other parts of her. She stopped at the water cooler, grabbed a cup, and bent down to fill it.

Bill and Edgar, as if pulled by invisible strings, both tilted their heads slightly to the side, just a little. Just enough to get a better look.

Then, like synchronized swimmers caught ogling by a shark, they both straightened up as Jessica stood and turned to face them. She raised one perfectly sculpted eyebrow, suspicion, or amusement, dancing in her eyes.

"I need out of this place," she said, brushing a stray lock of hair from her cheek. "Marty's working me to the bone lately."

Bill, mid-sip, nearly choked. He turned away, sputtering into his cup. Edgar bit his lip to hold in a grin, failing miserably.

"Yeah," Edgar stammered, "I mean, uh... yeah."

Bill wiped his mouth with the back of his hand. "Yeah, I can imagine. He's been calling you into his office *a lot* lately."

Jessica gave a tight, unreadable smile and sipped her water. For a moment, the tension hung between them.

Jessica stood there, casually sipping her water as the two guys nearby tried desperately, and obviously, to sneak glances at her ample assets. Their subtlety was about as effective as a neon sign in a blackout.

Finally, Jessica rolled her eyes so hard, it was a miracle they didn't roll out of their sockets. She turned on them with a sharp smile that was half amusement, half warning.

"Keep it in your pants," she said, voice dripping with enough sarcasm to drown a small office. Then she walked off, hips swaying as though teasing them one last time.

Bill was about to make some snarky comeback to Edgar when Janice appeared, dragging her reluctant kid, Dylan, by the hand like a tired Sherpa hauling a stubborn pack mule.

"Here, just drink some of this water," Janice snapped, clearly fed up with the boys' antics. Dylan yanked at her grip, desperate to escape.

"I don't want water. I want *something to eat*!" he whined, eyes wide and pleading.

Bill shot Edgar a look and rolled his eyes again like he was personally responsible for every office meltdown ever.

"Well, we don't have anything here," Janice muttered, as if stating the obvious to a toddler was an Olympic-level challenge.

Finally, Edgar piped up, voice tentative. "Actually... we got a new vending machine."

Janice shot him a glare that could curdle milk. "*Thank you, Edgar,*" she said, sharply.

"Yeah, Mom! I want something from the vending machine!" Dylan said, his voice rising with hopeful excitement.

The three of them turned down the hall toward the new contraption, a vending machine so strange, it looked like a prop from a sci-fi B-movie. All black, no pictures, no labels, just an ominous, glossy slab standing in stark contrast to the beige office walls.

Janice walked up and squinted at it, Dylan hovering at her side like a mini tornado.

"How does this thing *work*?" she muttered, genuinely puzzled.

Bill tilted his head, curiosity winning over his cynicism for the first time all morning. "Huh. When did we even get that?"

Edgar shrugged, eyes darting nervously between the machine and the hallway. "Not sure. I first saw it about thirty minutes ago."

Bill and Edgar stepped closer to Janice, peering at the vending machine with growing suspicion, like it might suddenly sprout legs and start chasing them.

Bill sighed, glancing down at the coin slot like it might answer some cosmic riddle.

"Well, can't be *too* much," he muttered, eyes narrowing. "It says twenty-five cents. Nothing these days costs that little. What's it gonna do, spit out a single piece of candy?" He smirked, half amused, half skeptical.

Edgar chuckled; well, tried to, but the laugh quickly twisted into another coughing fit that rattled his chest like a broken washing machine. Bill watched him for a moment before letting out an exaggerated sigh.

"Fine. I'll see what this stupid machine's got," he said, fishing a quarter out of his pocket.

With a theatrical flair, Bill slid the coin into the slot. "Come on, what do you have for me, you dumb glorified snack dispenser?" he muttered under his breath.

Suddenly, the machine's front panel flickered to life. Lights blinked and shimmered, swirling like on a slot machine in Vegas. The air buzzed with an electric hum as colors danced across the glossy black surface.

Then, with a smooth mechanical *whirr*, the entire front of the machine swung open like a secret door.

The trio leaned in, eyes wide, to see a single can of beer sitting deep inside, nestled in the back like a hidden treasure.

Everyone exchanged puzzled glances. The machine didn't look big enough to hold something *that* far back.

Bill's face broke into a grin that stretched ear to ear.

"Now *that's* what I'm talking about," he said, stepping forward. "This might just make this soul-sucking job a little more tolerable."

He reached inside, squeezing his broad shoulders through the opening, but as he did, the door slammed shut behind him with a *clang* that echoed down the hall.

Janice and Edgar jumped back, startled.

"What the hell just happened?!" Edgar shouted, eyes wide. "Get him out!"

Janice rushed forward, grabbing at the door, while Edgar tugged frantically on the handle, but it wouldn't budge, not an inch.

Panic flashed in Edgar's eyes as he pulled harder, ready to sprint for help, when suddenly, the door *clicked* open.

Out stepped... Bill?

Well, sort of.

This Bill was younger, *much* younger. The years had peeled away, replaced with lean muscle and toned abs that looked like they belonged on a fitness magazine cover. His beard was perfectly trimmed, and his hair was styled like some kind of runway model's.

"Uh... that was weird," Bill said, sounding annoyed as he dusted off his shirt. "The door shut, the beer disappeared, and I didn't get a damn thing for my twenty-five cents."

Janice, Edgar, and even Dylan stared at him, mouths slightly agape, wide-eyed like they'd just seen a ghost, or a damn vending machine miracle.

Bill raised an eyebrow, confused by the wide-eyed stares aimed at him.

"What the hell are you two looking at?" he asked, brushing imaginary lint off his shirt.

Then he frowned and tugged at the fabric. "What's wrong with this shirt? Did I stretch it or something?"

He took a step forward, and immediately had to snatch at his waistband as his pants started sliding down his hips.

"What in the actual hell?" he muttered, gripping the belt loops like his dignity depended on it.

Janice, still blinking like she'd just seen a unicorn eat her taxes, fished through her purse and pulled out a compact mirror. She flipped it open and held it up to him.

Bill stared into the reflection. His eyes went wide.

"Well, I'll be damned," he said slowly. "I look like my twenty-year-old self."

A grin spread across his face as he lifted his shirt to examine his torso, abs like sculpted marble, not a beer gut in sight.

"Would you look at *that*," he said, sounding both impressed and a little smug.

That was *exactly* the moment Jessica turned the corner.

"Marty wants to know why no one's at their..." she stopped mid-sentence. Her eyes landed on Bill's perfectly defined six-pack like they were magnets.

She blinked. Hard.

"Uh... who is *this*?" she asked, voice caught somewhere between intrigue and confusion.

Janice and Edgar stood frozen, still staring at the transformed version of Bill. For once, *Jessica* wasn't the center of attention, and she knew it.

She shifted her weight, arms crossed, a scowl tugging at her lips.

"Hello?" she said, her voice sharp enough to cut drywall. "Why am I being ignored?"

Neither Janice nor Edgar responded. Their eyes were locked on Bill; young, ripped, glowing-with-vitality Bill.

Bill, for his part, beamed. He ran a hand through his full head of hair and flashed a smile that hadn't seen daylight in over two decades.

"Oh, baby," he said, his voice smooth and dripping with newfound confidence, "there's no way we could ever ignore *you.*"

Jessica blinked, then *swooned*, ever so slightly.

Edgar's jaw dropped. Bill was flirting with Jessica.

And not the desperate kind. The *equal footing* kind. The *actual chance* kind.

And to Edgar's horror... it was working.

Jessica grinned and gave Bill a teasing wave as she sauntered down the hallway, hips in full hypnotic sway. She stopped at a door, glanced back, and motioned for him to follow.

Bill's grin widened into something feral. "Well... don't wait up," he said, then disappeared behind the door with her. The click of it closing echoed like a gunshot.

Edgar just stood there, stunned.

Bill was going to get a piece of Jessica.

The laws of the office universe were crumbling.

Panic and excitement surged in Edgar's chest. He fumbled into his pocket, his fingers searching desperately. His heart pounded.

Please let there be a quarter. Please, please, please...

His hand closed around cold metal. *Yes.* He almost cried.

"Oh thank goodness," he whispered, breathless, his voice trembling with relief.

He sprinted toward the vending machine, practically shaking as he bent down to slide the coin into the slot. But the quick motion jostled something in his lungs, he broke into a harsh coughing fit, hacking uncontrollably.

"Not now, dammit!" he croaked.

When it finally passed, he wiped his mouth, eyes watering, and shoved the quarter in like he was inserting a key into heaven's lock.

The machine came to life once more.

Lights flickered and the hum started. Colors danced across the sleek black surface like fireflies on a slot machine. Edgar stood straight, eyes wide, lips parted in anticipation.

He was about to get back *what he lost.*

This time, only half the front of the vending machine opened with a smooth *click*, like a high-tech refrigerator door. Cold air spilled out, and inside sat a single can, matte black, pulsing faintly with a soft blue glow.

Edgar tilted his head. The can looked sleek, otherworldly, and deeply unsettling in its simplicity.

"Huh. Okay... different than Bill's," he muttered, stepping forward.

He reached out slowly, fingertips brushing the surface. Nothing happened, there wasn't fanfare or a magical light show. Just... cold metal. He wrapped his fingers around the can and pulled it out. Across the label, in clean silver script, were the words:

LOST AND FOUND.

Edgar stared at it for a second, then shrugged and popped the tab. With a quiet hiss, the can opened, releasing a faint, citrusy scent that made his mouth water.

He lifted the can to his lips and drank.

It was... amazing. The best energy drink he'd ever tasted. Perfectly cold, smooth and sweet without being syrupy. As it slid down his throat, the world seemed to *slow*. Every sound stretched, every movement became sharper.

He bounced lightly on his heels, it felt like electricity running under his skin. His fingers tingled. Then his cheeks.

He reached up instinctively, rubbing at his face.

His hand came away dusted in white. Like powder.

Janice and Dylan both gasped.

"Oh my goodness," Janice whispered, eyes wide. "What's happening?"

"What's it *doing* to me?" Edgar asked, panic flickering in his voice.

Janice, without a word, dug into her purse and once again held up her compact mirror. Edgar leaned in and froze.

The skin on his face was flaking off in tiny, weightless pieces, like ashes from a dying fire, revealing smooth, healthy skin underneath. His complexion, once sickly and pale, was becoming radiant. Youthful, even.

For a long moment, he just stared.

Then he laughed. First a chuckle. Then a wild, relieved laugh that echoed down the hallway.

"I feel amazing!" he said, spinning once in place. "No shakes... no pain..."

He waited, almost instinctively, for the familiar cough to rattle up from his chest.

But it didn't come.

"I... I have my *health* back," he whispered, almost reverently. Then, louder, to no one and everyone: "I have my health back!"

He laughed again, louder this time. Joyful. Triumphant.

The door Jessica and Bill had disappeared behind suddenly *burst open* with a bang that made Janice and Dylan jump. Jessica stormed out, her face red with fury as she furiously buttoned up her blouse.

"You have *got* to be kidding me," she snapped, not even looking back. "How do you look like *that* and still... *ugh*!"

She huffed in frustration, then spun on her heel and marched off toward Marty's office, heels clicking like gunfire down the hallway.

Edgar blinked. "What the hell just happened?"

Bill stepped out sheepishly, looking bewildered and scratching the back of his head. "Man... I don't even know. There she was, *naked*. Like... incredible. A literal dream come true. And I just... couldn't."

Edgar tilted his head. "Couldn't what?"

Bill sighed and pointed downward. "*It*. Nothing happened. No reaction. Nada."

Edgar burst into laughter. "Wait, *seriously*? You're built like a Greek statue now and the plumbing doesn't work?!"

Bill looked down, brow furrowed, then glared at his crotch like it had personally betrayed him. "Yeah. I've never had that problem before. I've imagined that scenario a million times. And now? Nothing. Like a dead fish."

Edgar slapped him on the shoulder, grinning. "Ah, don't stress it, man. There'll be other chances. I mean, that's a lot of stress."

Bill gave his pants another annoyed tug. "Yeah, well... *you* better get your act together next time," he muttered under his breath to his disobedient anatomy.

Then he looked up and did a double take. "Whoa, look at you, Edgar! You look... amazing!"

Edgar grinned, his face glowing, eyes bright and jittering like a raccoon who found a Red Bull stash.

"Damn straight, I did!" Edgar said, bouncing lightly on his heels. "Popped a quarter in and *bam*! New me! I feel like I could run a marathon and not be winded at all!"

His speech was fast, words tumbling over each other like his mouth was trying to outrun his thoughts.

Bill laughed. "Still weird as hell, man. But yeah, you look good. Maybe *you'll* have better luck with Jessica than I did."

Janice wasn't listening.

She stood in front of the vending machine now, a quarter clenched tightly in her hand. Her eyes were locked on it like it was coaxing her forward.

Over the years, she'd let herself go. Not by choice, but due to not having the time to focus on fitness. Having a kid, working double shifts, then add in fast food in the car. She didn't have time to work out, or shop organic, or do yoga like those flawless office girls who never seemed to age.

She used to care about how she looked. She used to *feel* like a person.

Now she stood in front of this weird, humming machine, the same one that had made Bill young, made Edgar glow, and thought: *Why not me?*

Her thumb rubbed across the edge of the coin.

It was only twenty-five cents.

"Listen," Edgar said with a grin, "let's go talk to Jessica. I'm sure we can talk her into it again. I mean, let's not pretend she has any kind of morals or anything."

Bill considered for a moment, then nodded. "Yeah. You might be right. Let's go find her."

Edgar practically speed-walked off, Bill close behind, struggling to keep up.

Janice's eyes stayed glued to the vending machine. Her gaze glazed over as her thoughts drifted somewhere far away.

Finally, with a slow, deliberate motion, she shoved a quarter into the slot.

The machine ignited, lights flickering and whirring softly, like a whispering beast awakening.

But unlike for the others, the front didn't open. Instead, a single piece of paper slid out from the receipt slot.

Janice bent down and picked it up, fingers trembling slightly.

Printed at the top of the paper were the words:
Read me for what you have lost.
She hesitated, then began to read aloud.
Years slipped by like shadows, soft and slow,
Days of laughter, tears, and endless woe.
Cradling a child, dreams set aside,
Freedom traded for a mother's pride.
Time stretched thin, a fading song,
The world moved on, while she held strong.
Now a gift, from the lost and found
Whispers softly, without a sound:
I return to you, your freedom...

Janice smiled, a flicker of excitement warming her chest. *This is it,* she thought. *Finally, things will change.*

"Mommy?" Dylan's small voice pulled her from her thoughts.

She glanced down at herself, waiting, hoping to see the promised transformation. But her reflection didn't shift. Her body looked exactly the same: tired, worn, real.

That was odd.

The others had changed. Why hadn't *she*?

"Mommy!" Dylan's voice came again, louder now, edged with panic.

Janice spun around, and froze.

Her son was melting.

His little form blurred, his arms dripping, like he was a popsicle left out in the sun too long. His features sagged and dripped, pooling into a shimmering puddle on the floor.

"Dylan!" she screamed, lunging to grab him. But her hands passed through the liquid, grasping nothing but cold, glistening wetness.

The horrifying truth crashed down on her.

Her freedom had a price.

And she had *wished* her son away.

Janice wailed, staggering upright. *This was her doing. Her fault.*

Tears streamed down her face as she bolted through the hallway, the remnants of her son still dripping from her trembling hands.

The sharp *clack-clack* of heels echoed from another corridor as Jessica appeared, Marty trailing behind her like a shadow.

"What are you talking about? He just looks different," Marty said, irritation tightening his brow. "Does a new comb-over really mean nobody's working?"

Jessica sighed, biting her lip. *It's more than that,* she thought, memories of Bill's transformed body flashing through her mind. *He actually looks... good.*

The two stopped at the water cooler, eyes scanning the empty cubicles.

"Where is everyone?" Jessica asked quietly.

Marty shrugged, his annoyance unmasked. "I really don't know, Jessica."

His gaze flicked to the mysterious vending machine, its sleek black surface glowing faintly in the dull office light.

"Oh, good," he muttered, reaching into his pocket and tossing a quarter to Jessica like a command. "I don't have time for this. Get me a drink. Meet me back in my office."

Without waiting for a reply, he turned on his heel and strode confidently down the hall toward his office.

Jessica stood silently for a moment, arms crossed, lips pursed in an annoyed pout. She gave Marty a lazy salute as he walked off, muttering under her breath, "The things I do for a promotion. Can't *wait* to be done with that loser."

She rolled her eyes and sauntered over to the vending machine, hips swaying like she was walking a catwalk instead of the breakroom floor.

"Alright, vending machine," she said with a sigh. "How the hell do I pick something from you?"

She stared at the smooth black surface, no buttons, no glass window, no visible options.

She shrugged. "Whatever. I hope he gets something *awful.*"

With a dramatic flair, she shoved the quarter into the slot.

The machine *rumbled*, louder than it should have. Lights flickered violently. The whole thing vibrated like a jet engine warming up.

Jessica stepped back. "Uh... the hell?"

Then, *click*, the front creaked open.

Inside wasn't soda. There weren't any snacks.

It was treasure.

Diamond necklaces shimmered like stars under soft white light. Ruby-studded rings sat in little velvet trays. The inside of the machine looked more like a high-end jewelry vault than anything remotely logical.

Jessica tilted her head as she scanned the items, then glanced around the office.

"No cameras?" she said with a grin. "Well then... looks like someone forgot to lock the vault."

She smirked to herself, eyes sparkling, and stepped inside.

The moment her foot crossed the threshold...

SLAM.

The door snapped shut like the jaws of a beast.

On the front of the door, words began to form. Slowly, the machine etched her fate one letter at a time until it read:

You played the game, you broke the rules,
Danced through years with thieves and fools.
You traded truth for charm and skin,
And laughed while letting darkness in.
But deep beneath the painted face,
A child's heart still held its place.
No need for guilt, no need for shame...
The path now ends where you became.
Begin once more, a softer start...
Your innocence, returned in part.

The vending machine hissed.

Then, with a mechanical shudder, the door creaked open.

The treasure was gone.

Both jewels... and flesh.

Where sparkling diamonds once sat, there now lay a baby girl, wrapped snugly in a carrier. Her soft skin glowed in the vending machine's pale light, a tiny rattle clutched in her hand as she giggled and kicked with innocent delight.

Behind a nearby doorframe, Janice peeked out, eyes wide and bloodshot.

Mascara streaked down her cheeks in trembling rivers. Her breath hitched as she saw the child.

For a moment, with just a flicker of impossible hope, her broken mind whispered, *Dylan?*

She stepped forward. Slowly. Carefully.

Her hands reached down, trembling as she lifted the baby into her arms. The child looked up at her with wide, unknowing eyes, and cooed again.

Janice marveled at the tiny face. The warm weight in her arms. She glanced around the empty office, confused.

There was no one.

No sign of another parent. No note.

Who would leave a baby here... in this cursed machine?

Then the machine let out a sharp, *angry beep.*

SLAM!

The door snapped shut with a violent bang that echoed through the room like a gunshot.

Janice screamed, clutching the child to her chest, stumbling back. Her breath came in panicked sobs as she turned and ran, her footsteps slapping across the linoleum.

She didn't look back.

She just ran.

Out of the room.

Out of the building.

Out of the nightmare.

And in her arms...

Jessica.

Born anew.

Innocent.

Unknowing.

The vending machine sat silently in the hallway, its surface dark and still. It waited.

An hour passed. Not a whisper. Not a breath.

Then, footsteps.

"Heh... Jessica? Where the hell is my soda?" Marty's voice echoed down the corridor, followed by the *stomp stomp stomp* of angry loafers.

He marched into the break room, his face already flushed with irritation.

The room was empty. Deserted.

He turned in a slow circle, frowning. "Where is *everyone?*" he muttered. "This is ridiculous."

Marty's eyes darted from one hallway to the next. He was going to have cameras installed. Hell, he *should've* done it months ago.

"Janice? Bill?" he barked. Nothing. Just the hum of the air conditioner and the low buzz of flickering fluorescent lights.

"Unbelievable," he huffed.

Shaking his head, Marty walked over to the vending machine. He fished out a quarter and held it up to the slot.

"They think they can slack off on *my* watch? I'll have HR crawling up their asses by noon."

He pressed the edge of the coin to the slot...

"Mr. Marty..."

A frail voice came from the cubicles behind him.

Marty froze.

An old man stepped into view. His back was slightly hunched, his face wrinkled and sunken. His clothes hung off him like they didn't quite fit anymore.

He looked familiar, barely.

"Edgar?" Marty squinted.

"Yes... Mr. Marty."

"What the hell happened to you?"

Edgar didn't answer at first. He just looked at the vending machine, his expression distant and hollow.

"The machine," he said softly. "It gave me energy... but it stole time. Sped up my life cycle, I think. I can feel it. I've aged *years* in an hour."

His tired eyes shifted, locking onto the coin halfway in the machine's slot.

His voice cracked as he shouted:

"*Marty, don't put that coin in!*"

Marty scoffed. "Oh, come *on*, Edgar. You and Bill are pulling some elaborate prank, huh? Gonna get a good laugh out of the old boss falling for it?"

He sneered.

"Nice try."

And with that, he shoved the coin in.

Click.

The vending machine blinked to life.

Lights flared. Gears turned. The whole unit began to *shake* violently, like it was waking from a nightmare.

Edgar stumbled backward, eyes wide with terror.

"Marty, *get away from it!*" he cried.

But Marty just smirked.

Until he heard it.

A *low rumble* deep inside the machine. A groan. A pulse. Something... alive.

Something waiting.

Marty slowly turned to face the vending machine.

Its lights glowed faint red.

Edgar took another shaky step back, horror plain in his eyes.

With a soft *click*, the machine door creaked open, just an inch.

Marty furrowed his brow and leaned in, curious. He reached out and gripped the edge of the door.

With a slow pull, it opened...

Only about a foot.

Then.

BANG!

The door *exploded* outward.

A woman's form launched from the darkness inside, screaming as she tackled him to the floor.

Marty stumbled back, falling hard onto his spine as the figure landed on top of him with a primal shriek.

Her face.

Familiar.

Pale.

Eyes wide with fury and betrayal.

"*Thought I was gone, did you, Marty?!*" she howled. "*What did you tell them? Huh? What did you say?*"

Her voice cracked like thunder. Her hands were wrapped around his collar.

"*Do they know you killed me?*" she screamed, shaking him violently. "*Your poor wife... last May?*"

Marty's mouth opened in a silent gasp.

"*You buried me under the cabin like a dog!*" she shrieked, teeth bared. "*Like I didn't mean a thing!*"

She yanked the pen from his shirt pocket, one of those cheap clicky ones he always chewed on, and drove it into his chest with manic fury.

Over and over.

Marty tried to fight, to roll away, but his screams were swallowed by her laughter.

Sharp, unhinged, echoing off the sterile office walls.

Edgar turned away, unable to look.

When the silence returned, it was cold and absolute.

The vending machine's lights dimmed again.

On its screen, glowing in soft, eerie white, were words that hadn't been there before.

We always chase what we've lost,
While ignoring what we have.
But some things lost
Should never return.
Three years later...

Donavin laughed as he wandered out of the restroom, wiping his hands on the sides of his khakis like a man who'd given up on the paper towel dispenser years ago.

He glanced over his shoulder. "Stan, you're a riot. You know I don't believe a damn word you say half the time."

Stan followed with a smug grin, clearly proud of whatever inappropriate joke he'd just dropped.

"You're gonna get fired for saying that kind of stuff one of these days," Donavin added, shaking his head.

Stan shrugged, unfazed. "Getting fired from this place would be the highlight of my life."

Then he stopped.

Brows lifted. Finger raised.

"Hey... when did we get *that?*"

Donavin paused and looked.

Standing in front of them was an odd-looking vending machine.

FOUR

THE ONES WHO STAYED BEHIND

Delilia Thomas stopped at the doorway.

She was only twelve, but fear didn't care how young she was. Her wide eyes stared into the dim room ahead. The door was open. Always open.

She hated this place.

This was where it showed up.

The creature.

It terrified her.

Her older sister said it wasn't the only one. Every house in town had them, she said. Every single one.

Delilia's family was lucky they had only one. Some families had five. Five invisible things living in their homes like unwelcome guests.

She shivered.

Still, Mother sent her to get the cookware. Of course, it was in that room. Always was.

Delilia didn't know why she was so scared. People had studied the creatures, tested them. Said you couldn't touch them. Said they couldn't hurt you. Said most of the time, the creatures couldn't even see you.

But sometimes, Delilia felt like this one could.

Standing in the doorway, it felt like the room was already full. Like she was stepping into someone else's space.

Finally, she took a deep breath and stepped inside.

Her eyes scanned left and right. It looked safe. Maybe.

Her feet moved slow and careful. The shadows clung to the walls, far too dark for midday. Every corner felt heavy.

She reached for the pan.

Her fingers touched the handle, but it slipped right through her grasp and crashed to the floor with a sharp metallic clatter.

She froze and gasped, eyes wide.

Across the room, something moved.

A shape, broad and tall, rose up from the darkness. It looked like a man. But it wasn't.

Its head tilted to the side, curious. An eyebrow lifted, a gesture far too human.

Delilia's blood turned to ice.

The thing was massive. Towering. Solid. And it was coming toward her.

Slow. Deliberate. Haunting.

She stumbled back and landed hard on her bottom. Her eyes never left the creature as it shuffled closer, dragging its weight like something half-asleep or half-dead.

It saw her.

It really saw her.

Panic surged in her chest. It was going to eat her. She knew it. Every instinct screamed to run.

But her body stayed frozen.

The creature glanced at the cabinet where the pan had been. Then slowly lowered its head, locking its gaze back onto hers.

And it crouched.

Long, bony fingers stretched toward her like spider legs.

She snapped out of it.

Twisting, she scrambled onto all fours, and bolted out of the room, heart pounding like thunder in her ears.

She had no pan in her hand and there was no way she was going back in there.

Mother would have to figure something else out for dinner.

That night, they ate skewered meats instead of the stew Mother had planned. The pan still lay on the floor in that cursed room, and Mother was too busy to fetch it herself.

She sighed and said, "Fine, Delilia."

Dinner was pleasant enough. The family ate their fill, shared stories, and laughed under the warm glow of the lantern. Then, one by one, they drifted off to bed.

Delilia curled up tight under her blanket.

She'd told Mother about the creature, the way it looked at her, how it moved. But Mother just laughed and brushed it off.

"There's no such thing as monsters," she said. "Even if there are, just ignore them. They'll leave you alone."

But Delilia couldn't shake the image. Couldn't stop replaying how it rose from the shadows, how it reached for her.

Her sister was already asleep across the room, breathing slow and steady. Clutching the same stuffed animal she'd had since she was three. Delilia thought that was funny. Who needed a stuffed animal at this age anyway?

She stared at the ceiling.

She wanted to sleep too. She really did. But her mind raced, building monsters in every dark corner.

She pulled the covers tight around her neck and closed her eyes, willing herself to relax.

Then, a sound.

Just outside the bedroom door.

Her eyes snapped open.

She turned slowly toward the door.

There it was.

The creature.

Lumbering past, silent as death. Its massive form blotting out the hallway light.

Then it stopped.

And turned.

Its head tilted, and it looked straight into the room.

Straight at her.

Delilia didn't breathe. Didn't blink.

She froze.

She wanted to scream. To whisper. To shake her sister awake and warn her.

But she didn't dare.

One sound or even one movement was all it would take. She knew it would find her.

So instead, Delilia pulled the blanket up tighter, until only her eyes peeked out. Her breath came in shallow gasps as she fought to stay silent.

The creature stepped inside the room.

It paused just past the doorway and didn't move for a long moment. Then slowly, it turned its head and began to scan the space.

It looked... curious. Perhaps a bit sorrowful.

Like this was the first time it had really seen the room.

Its dark eyes wandered from wall to wall, studying everything. The bookshelf. The toy chest. Her sister's pile of blankets.

It didn't seem to see her.

Maybe I'm hidden, she thought. *Maybe I'm safe.*

She prayed.

The creature lumbered across the room toward the closet. It opened the door with surprising gentleness, peering inside like it had all the time in the world.

It moved a few things around. Examined a stuffed animal. Picked up an old pair of boots.

Then, it put them back.

Delilia's heart thudded so hard, she thought it might burst.

Still, the creature didn't look at her.

She kept repeating the words in her head like a mantra:

Please don't see me. Please don't see me. Please don't see me...

The creature turned toward the door. Then stopped.

Its head shifted slightly. Its gaze fell on Delilia's sister.

Then it started to move.

Its footsteps were slow, heavy. Intentional, even.

Lumbering toward the bed.

Delilia's breath caught in her throat. Her body screamed to move, to shout, to do something. But she couldn't. She was frozen, watching it approach her sister like a shadow with teeth.

The creature stopped at the edge of the bed.

It looked down on her.

Her sister lay curled up, clutching a stuffed animal to her face. Breathing soft and steady. Peaceful. Completely unaware the danger was inches away.

The creature reached down.

Its fingers stretched out, long, thin, impossibly slow. Mere inches from her sister's face.

Delilia's heart pounded against her ribs like a war drum.

Do something, she screamed inside. *Say something!*

But just then, a thud echoed down the hallway.

Delilia flinched.

The creature froze.

It turned its head slowly toward the sound, alert but not panicked. Curious. Like a predator interrupted during a hunt.

Her mother must be up. Maybe she needed to use the bathroom? Normal life brushing up against nightmares.

The creature straightened.

It peered both ways down the hall, then slowly, cautiously, stepped out of the room and disappeared.

Delilia didn't wait.

She threw off her blanket, bolted across the room, and dove into bed beside her sister.

Startled, her sister groaned and cracked an eye open.

"What are you doing?" she mumbled.

Delilia wrapped her arms tight around her sister. "I'm scared," she whispered. "I want to sleep with you."

Her sister sighed, shifting under the blankets. "Fine. But don't steal all the covers."

Delilia buried her face in her sister's shoulder, the warmth, the safety, the realness of her.

After a while, the fear eased just enough.

Her eyelids grew heavy. Shadows softened.

Finally, sleep came.

Morning arrived soft and golden through the windows, like nothing had happened.

The family moved through their day, breakfast, chores, quiet talks.

At the table, Delilia leaned close to her sister and whispered, "It came into our room last night. It almost touched you."

Her sister raised an eyebrow, smirking. "Oh no, did the big shadow monster try to braid my hair?"

"I'm serious!" Delilia hissed. "It was right there. Inches away."

Her sister snorted. "Delilia, it doesn't want us. If it did, it would've done something by now."

Delilia wasn't so sure.

"Some kids at school," her sister went on, "say the creatures are spirits. Like ghosts. That's why they can't touch us."

Delilia frowned, stirring her cereal. "But spirits can touch people. They take souls in those stories. Drag kids away."

Her sister rolled her eyes. "Yeah, in stories. These ones just watch. That's all."

But Delilia felt that cold weight deep in her chest.

She'd seen the way it looked at her. The way it reached for her sister.

It wasn't just watching.

It wasn't done yet.

"Kento, from down the street, is missing," Delilia said quietly.

Her sister didn't even look up. "Kento's not missing. He went to visit family out of town."

Delilia blinked. "Are you sure?"

"Yeah. He's been talking about it for, like, a week now."

Delilia tried to remember if she'd heard anything like that. Kento was older. They didn't really talk. He was always off doing something "cool" with the older kids. Maybe he did say something. Maybe.

She huffed and looked away as her sister went back to brushing her doll's hair like it was the most important thing in the world.

That night, everything seemed normal.

First came dinner, then there were the Chores, and once again lights out.

But as she lay in her bed, Delilia's mind raced. Replaying every detail.

Was Kento gone? What about the creature standing over her sister? It was mere inches from her face.

Her sister said she was overthinking it. Maybe she was.

But what if she wasn't?

She needed to know.

No, she told herself. She needed to see.

But not with her sister in the room. Not again.

She waited until the house was silent. Until the creaks and hums of night settled into stillness.

She glanced over at her sister, curled up and fast asleep, but without her stuffed animal. She'd spent half the day stomping around, whining about it missing, insisting Delilia had taken it.

Delilia denied it, of course.

She didn't want that stupid thing. That was for babies.

Still... the accusation stung.

Then she slipped quietly from bed.

Careful not to wake her sister, Delilia padded into the hallway. The wooden floor was cool against her bare feet.

She stopped in front of the door.

This was the room where it had appeared.

The air felt colder here, like she was walking through snow.

She stared at the dark doorway, her hand hovering near the edge.

Her heart pounded hard against her ribs.

She was scared.

But she didn't turn back.

She didn't want to be eaten.

Not that she was completely sure that was what it did... but she wasn't ruling it out either.

Still, curiosity pressed harder than fear.

Slowly, Delilia slipped inside the dark room.

It smelled faintly of dust, old wood, and something strong, like maybe vinegar.

The pan was gone from the floor. It had found its way back on the shelf.

That made her skin crawl.

She breathed quietly, careful not to make a sound, and looked toward the spot where the creature had risen before.

And there it was.

The creature's shape stretched out on the couch like a sleeping bear.

Its chest rose and fell slowly. Rhythmic. It was almost peaceful.

In front of it sat a gin bottle, half-empty and sweating with condensation.

It drinks?

Her heartbeat thundered in her ears, but she moved closer. One cautious step at a time. Eyes darting, feet silent.

She glanced around the room, the details sharper now, alien and familiar all at once.

And then she saw it.

A newspaper. Folded, sitting neat on the coffee table.

She hadn't noticed it before.

She'd never spent more than a minute or two in this room before running scared. But now, up close, something about that paper pulled at her.

She leaned in.

Her eyes scanned the words. Then moved to the pictures. Finally, they rested on the headline.

Her fingers trembled as they reached for it.

Maybe this newspaper was the key to the creatures' appearances?

Maybe it was what tethered the spirit here, something unfinished. Something keeping it from moving on.

Delilia's eyes scanned the faded print.

Sixty People Killed in Freak Gas Leak, the headline screamed.

Her stomach dropped.

She read on. Details about an accident, some kind of gas leak in a residential neighborhood. The deaths were quick. There was no warning. Entire homes of people were killed while they slept in the night.

Her breath caught when she hit the end.

Below the article, a grid of black-and-white photos. Victims.

So many faces.

Her eyes darted across them, desperate to find him, the man on the couch. Maybe this was how he died. Maybe this was his story.

Then she found it.

Not the man.

Herself.

Her fingers trembled as they hovered over a name, printed in small, cold type.

Delilia Thompson.

She stared, frozen in place.

Her heart hammered in her chest.

That was her name. Exactly her name.

The article said she was dead.

But... she wasn't.

Was she?

Her eyes flicked down the list again.

Delilia Thompson.

Then another name.

Marie Thompson, her mother.

No...

Then Anna Thompson, her sister.

Her breath hitched.

And further down... Kento Alvarez.

Her knees nearly gave out. No, no, no...

Her mind spun, desperate to find a foothold, but it was like trying to catch water with your bare hands. Everything was slipping away.

They were all there.

Every one of them.

Dead.

The article didn't lie. This wasn't a joke. There was no exaggeration.

Sixty people lost in one night. One quiet neighborhood wiped clean.

Her eyes flicked back to the couch.

The man.

Still sleeping. Still breathing slow.

And now... there was a flicker of something behind his face.

She knew him. Her heart broke a bit.

Recognition crawling through her mind like a memory trying to wake from a coma.

That's...

That's my daddy.

Not a monster.

Not a ghost.

Just a man. The man who wasn't there the night everything ended.

He was on a work trip and survived the tragedy, he wasn't reaching for her sister to hurt her.

He wasn't prowling the halls to haunt them.

He was living in the house where it all fell apart.

Holding on to whatever scraps he had left.

She looked again, the haunted eyes, the bottle of gin, the way each step through the house seemed to break him into a thousand quiet pieces.

The night before... when he reached out to her sister...

He wasn't reaching for her.

He was reaching for the stuffed animal clutched in her arms.

A relic of a life lost.

A child gone.

A piece of what he'd once loved.

Tears welled in Delilia's eyes and slipped down her cheeks, but she didn't know if they were real.

Do ghosts even cry?

She sank to her knees before the man who'd once been her whole world.

And for the first time in this strange, silent afterlife... she understood.

She was the ghost.

And he was the one haunted.

Her mind spun, reality unraveling like an old sweater snagged on a nail.

"Daddy?" she whispered, her voice barely more than a breath.

The word cracked something wide open inside her chest, raw and aching.

She wanted to scream and cry. To grab him, and shake him, to tell him she was right here ... that he wasn't alone. Not really.

That she'd never left.

But she couldn't.

Not anymore.

She moved closer, hands shaking at her sides, eyes burning with tears she couldn't tell were real or not.

He stirred.

Just a flicker.

A subtle turn of his head, like he sensed something.

She held her breath.

"Daddy..." she said again, voice trembling this time.

His eyes opened.

They were tired-looking. Bloodshot and full of sorrow that didn't fade, the kind of pain that settles in your bones like a permanent scar.

He looked around, not at her, but through her, past her.

Then his gaze landed on the stuffed animal lying on the floor.

The one her sister clutched.

The one she'd once loved.

Slowly, he reached down and picked it up. Cradled it in his big, calloused hands.

His shoulders shook.

And for the first time in her death... she saw him cry.

Delilia stepped closer, her ghost-light form flickering faintly in the dim room.

"I'm still here," she whispered. "Watching. Keeping you safe."

She reached out, fingers trembling, but they passed through his hand like smoke.

Still, he paused.

He looked up.

Right at her.

His brows knitted, as if he could almost see her.

Almost.

And for a heartbeat, he smiled.

A fragile spark of warmth in a storm of grief.

Delilia smiled too, tears slipping silently down her cheeks.

She didn't need to scream anymore.

He knew.

He felt her.

And that was enough.

Quietly, she climbed onto the couch, curling up beside her daddy's weary form.

His eyes drifted shut again, a single tear tracing down his cheek as his chest hitched with a quiet sob.

He missed them. His girls were his whole world.

But somehow... he felt them still here. Watching him. Staying close to him.

It wouldn't be easy. Grief never was.

But he would find his way back up from the depths.

He had to.

For them.

And maybe, someday, in a distant future, they'd be together again.

Until then, he'd be strong.

Because that's what they would've wanted.

Delilia rested her head against his chest, her ghostly arms wrapping around him as she closed her eyes.

She felt safe, like he was the one protecting her.

But the truth was... she was the one saving him.

And she would keep saving him.

Every night.

Until he didn't need her anymore.

FIVE

THE VELDT EFFECT

Davis lifted his fork to his mouth, eyes drifting across the room. This was his favorite restaurant. He used to think it was his family's favorite, too. But here he was, eating alone.

Well, technically not alone.

His wife and two kids sat across from him, each one glued to a glowing screen, faces lit with that eerie digital flicker. None of them had looked up since they'd sat down.

He shoveled a forkful of eggs into his mouth and chewed slowly.

"How's your food, dear?" he asked.

No response.

"Honey?"

His wife's eyes finally darted up, dazed like she'd just been yanked out of a dream. "Huh?" she said, blinking.

"Your food," he repeated. "How is it?"

She glanced down at her untouched plate, like she'd forgotten it was there. "Uh... uhm... it's good."

He nodded. "I'm happy to hear it."

And that was the meal.

It was always like this now.

Davis looked around the restaurant. Table after table, the same scene played out. Not just his family, but other families, couples, groups of friends, and even people on dates. All of them were silent. All of them staring into the tiny black mirrors in their hands.

Like worshippers at a digital altar.

The meal finally ended. Davis stood and led his near-zombie family to the register to pay.

They waited.

The woman behind the counter didn't notice them, her eyes were locked onto her phone, swiping left and right, darting across the tiny screen as if the outside world had ceased to exist. She was so absorbed; it was as if the family in front of her were ghosts.

Davis cleared his throat.

She glanced up, startled. "Oh! Hello there!" she chirped, her voice dripping with fake cheer.

He didn't respond. He knew the truth, everyone was irritated now, annoyed that reality had the nerve to interrupt their digital fix.

They left the restaurant. The drive home was silent.

No conversation, or music. Just the faint hum of tires on pavement and the glow of screens lighting his passengers' faces. His wife and kids remained nose-deep in their devices, watching life pass by through a five-inch window, oblivious to the real world just beyond the glass.

When they pulled into the driveway, Davis got out.

He waited.

But nobody followed.

They just sat there in the parked car, still scrolling, still tapping, as if the drive never ended. They hadn't even noticed they were home.

This wasn't the first time.

There was one night, weeks ago, when he'd gone inside, made a drink, watched a movie, and gone to bed. It wasn't until hours later, well past midnight, that they finally came in. Wordless and blank-eyed.

As if they'd wandered in from some other realm entirely.

He reached up and knocked on the car window. There was no response.

He tried again, this time harder. Slowly, all three heads turned toward him. Eyes took a moment to register recognition, like old computers booting up. Then, in eerie unison, they reached down and opened their doors.

One by one, they climbed out and followed him toward the house in silence.

As they approached, the front panel chimed softly.

"Welcome, Davis Anderson."

The door slid open, and the lights flickered on. The house was fully automated now, biometric scans, adaptive lighting, even scent customization. Davis had been against it. Why couldn't people just flip a damn switch? But his wife insisted.

So here they were.

As the door slid shut behind them, the kids peeled off without a word, disappearing into opposite ends of the house. He didn't need to guess where they were headed, the blankness in their eyes told him everything. More screen time. Always more screen time.

His wife lingered by the door, struggling to kick off her boots while staring down at her phone. Davis bent down and pulled them off for her.

She didn't thank him. Just shuffled over to the couch, curled up under a blanket, and started scrolling again.

Davis poured himself a drink, sat down, and soon drifted into a restless sleep.

He woke up to something strange.

Conversation.

Not the monotone *uh-huh*s of distracted replies. Actual words. He even heard laughter. For a moment, he thought he was dreaming.

He wiped his eyes and followed the voices into the kitchen.

His wife and kids were at the dinner table, animated, smiling, talking. Their eyes were bright with excitement as they chatted over each other like they used to, years ago.

"What's all the excitement?" Davis asked, blinking at the scene.

His wife jumped up and rushed over, her face alight.

"Davis, did you see? A new company, Veldt Inc., they just dropped an app! They say you can do anything on it. Anything, Davis!"

That brief flicker of hope in his chest, he'd thought maybe, just maybe they'd snapped out of it, snuffed out instantly. Another app. Another escape from the real world.

"Is that so?" he asked flatly. "Is that something we really need?"

Her expression darkened.

"Of course it is, Davis. I do enough around here. Why wouldn't you want things to be easier for me?"

Ah. There it was. Her go-to rebuttal. He could've mouthed it along with her.

He nodded, defeated. "Of course, dear."

"Yes, Daddy! It comes out tomorrow!" his daughter beamed. "It's going to change everything! You can watch people's home cameras, if they let you, and you can have your kitchen sync with meals other families are cooking!"

His son nodded eagerly. "It's going to be so exciting, Dad!"

Davis smiled, though something twisted in his gut. Still, it was hard to deny the warmth he felt seeing his kids look at him. They were talking to him. Actually *engaged*. Like he existed again.

"Is that so? Well," he said, keeping his voice light, "let's just not get too caught up in it. There's still a life outside those screens, remember?"

They both nodded absentmindedly, already slipping back into their devices.

He sighed and retreated to his office upstairs to begin his workday.

All day long, it was the same. From coworkers to clients, everyone was buzzing about the app. Veldt Inc. was the topic on every tongue, in every chat window. Strangely, it was the most conversation he'd had with his colleagues in months.

And yet, that ever-present sense of dread gnawed at the back of his mind.

Then the day arrived.

The world seemed to stop.

Phones were lifted like sacred relics. Faces turned downward as the light of the real world dimmed.

Davis wandered into the kitchen. His family sat at the table, silent, eyes glazed over.

"Honey? Is dinner ready?" he asked.

No answer.

He tried again. "Hun?"

She looked up, startled, like waking from a dream. "Huh?"

"Dinner?"

Still dazed, she shook her head and turned back to her phone. A few swipes later, the kitchen appliances beeped to life and began preparing food.

Davis stared at them as machines chopped, boiled, and stirred. All without her lifting a finger.

He leaned over her shoulder to see what she was doing.

She was playing a game.

It was a cooking simulator of some kind.

Her finger moved across the screen, moving items from here to there. She digitally prepared a meal all while the actual machines cooked for her for real offscreen.

He shook his head and stepped across to his son, peering over his shoulder.

A video was playing of a monkey stealing bananas from vendors, tossing peels everywhere. The narrator warned about the end of the world due to excessive littering.

Davis blinked. *What?*

He moved to his daughter, hoping for something different.

She was watching a live nanny-cam feed. Onscreen, children played in a hyper-advanced room that morphed to their will. He'd read about those luxury families, rich tech-heads giving their kids augmented environments.

In this feed, the kids had transformed the room into a wide savanna.

Lions lounged in the digital grass.

Lions.

They were realistic and massive and watched everything around them.

The kids giggled as one lion prowled close to them, brushing up against their legs.

Davis tilted his head.

What kind of child wants that for a playroom?

Then again... who wouldn't want to pet a lion safely?

He stared at the screen a moment longer, unease settling like a stone in his stomach.

Davis shivered. Something about the way those lions moved... it felt like they could see him.

He grabbed his dinner and ate in silence. Across the table, his family remained frozen, none of them bothered to dish up their food. They didn't take a single bite.

That unsettled him.

Tomorrow, he told himself. Tomorrow I'll say something. Ensure they make better choices.

He brushed his teeth, got ready for bed, and drifted off to sleep.

The morning arrived too early.

Davis rolled over, expecting to see his wife next to him. Her side of the bed was untouched. Strange. Even if she stayed up late staring at her phone, she usually made her way to bed at some point.

He slipped on his slippers and padded down the stairs.

They were still at the dinner table.

All three of them were staring at their screens.

They hadn't moved. Dark circles ringed their eyes, their postures stiff and unnatural. Had they been there all night?

Davis's stomach tightened. This was spiraling out of control. But he wasn't ready for another argument, not yet. So, he let it go.

Upstairs, he logged in to work and sat at his desk.

The entire day went by with no messages, meetings, or clients.

None of his coworkers were online.

It was... quiet.

Too quiet.

The entire day passed like that, an empty inbox and a blinking cursor.

When it was finally over, Davis made himself a sandwich and ate it alone. He didn't hear a sound from the rest of the house. There was a lack of footsteps, conversation or sounds in general. He assumed they were all in their rooms.

He poured a drink and settled into the couch, trying to unwind.

Eventually, he trudged back upstairs. His wife was lying in bed, staring at her phone. At least she was there.

He slipped under the covers and leaned in to kiss her goodnight. She didn't flinch. Her eyes never looked up to acknowledge him at all.

With a sigh, he picked up his tablet and started looking into the app himself.

Veldt Inc.

A new kind of connection.

Show yourself what you most desire.

It was supposedly designed to relax you. To make you "comfortable with the present." Every user experienced something uniquely tailored for you.

The company's profit model was based on active users. The longer you stayed logged in, the more they made.

Davis narrowed his eyes.

"Of course they do," he muttered.

He set the tablet on the nightstand and turned out the light.

Sleep came quickly, but not peacefully.

Davis woke and looked over at his wife. She wasn't asleep. She was looking at her phone.

Did she sleep at all? He wasn't sure. Her eyes were still dark and she had a tired look about her.

"How did you sleep, hun?" he asked curiously.

She didn't respond.

Shaking his head, he got up and made himself ready for work.

The day was uneventful again. Not a single client called in. His coworkers, once again, were nowhere to be seen. He was beginning to worry. Maybe this app was far more than he thought it was.

Davis's day finished, and he logged off, making his way down the stairs to get some dinner.

His family was at the dinner table.

Davis paused and looked at them.

Was it just him, or did they seem... skinnier? For that matter, had he seen them eat at all in the past couple of days?

They all had dark circles under their eyes.

Have the kids not slept at all either?

This had to stop.

"We need to have a talk," he said.

The three once again didn't look up from their phones.

His voice rose to an angry level.

"Put those away and pay attention to me, dammit!"

But still, nothing.

Finally, he moved forward, grabbing each of their phones out of their hands.

Their eyes flashed up to meet his, anger instantly evident.

"What do you think you're doing, Davis?"

The kids began to yell.

"Dad! Why did you do that!"

He held the phones in his hand and stared at them all.

"I'm trying to have a conversation with my family, but you're all too engrossed in these devices. I think you need a cleanse. No phones till tomorrow."

His wife looked like she was about to have a nervous breakdown.

"Davis, you have got to be kidding me. You want to create extra work for me?" she nearly screamed.

"Nope. Not this time, Samantha. I'm holding on to these till tomorrow. I'd advise you all, get some rest, and some food in you."

Davis went up to his room and sat on the edge of the bed. For once, there was something comforting in the silence, no flickering light beside him, no faint sound of mindless scrolling. Just stillness. He looked forward to finally falling asleep without that pale, ghostly glow haunting the other side of the mattress.

With a quiet huff, he shoved the phones into his nightstand drawer and shut it firmly. Out of sight. Out of mind.

He lay back and stared at the ceiling, the pillow cool against his head. From downstairs, he could still hear them, muffled voices, raised slightly. There was a sharpness to them. Anger, maybe? Most definitely frustration. Possibly even crying. It was hard to tell.

But it didn't matter. He knew this was the right thing and they needed this. A break, a reset. Even if they couldn't see it yet.

Eventually, his eyes closed and the darkness welcomed him.

Sometime in the night, Davis woke with a familiar pressure in his bladder. He blinked, confused for a moment by the stillness. Then he turned to the other side of the bed, and frowned.

It was empty.

His wife's side was untouched. The sheets hadn't been pulled back and there was no trace of her presence at all.

He sighed. Maybe she was still upset and had decided to crash on the couch. He'd check in a moment, after the bathroom.

Once finished, he stepped out into the hallway and walked toward the stairs. That was when he saw it.

A soft glow.

It spilled faintly from the kitchen like candlelight, but colder, flickering. Familiar.

Was that the glow of a screen?

Davis froze. He narrowed his eyes, then turned back to the bedroom, his heart beginning to race. He went straight to the nightstand and yanked open the drawer.

It was completely empty.

The phones were gone.

Someone had taken them.

His pulse thudded in his ears.

This ends now, he thought. If he had to smash every one of those screens into fragmented shards, so be it.

He stormed back toward the stairs, ready to confront them, but stopped short.

The hammer.

He needed his hammer.

Where had he left it? Right, the spare room closet. He spun on his heel and marched down the hall, his bare feet padding against the floor.

He opened the spare room door and stepped inside. Moonlight poured through the window, casting long shadows against the wall. The closet stood ahead, door slightly ajar.

He opened it fully and reached in, fingers closing around the wooden handle of the hammer.

As he turned to leave...

He froze.

His wife stood in the doorway, framed by the dim hallway light.

And beside her... were the kids.

All three of them.

Their faces were far too calm.

Samantha smiled but it never reached her eyes.

With a tap of her screen, the closet door shut and clicked.

The lock engaged with a mechanical finality, locking him in the closet.

"Samantha," Davis called through the door, confused, his voice hoarse with disbelief. "What are you doing?"

She looked down at her phone and tapped something else.

"You need a time-out, Davis," she said smoothly. "We'll let you out tomorrow. Once you understand how this is going to work."

"Samantha, this isn't funny!" he shouted, slamming his palm against the door. "Let me out!"

There came no answer, just silence.

Seven years later...

The man walked through the wreckage of the building, boots crunching over shattered glass and scorched debris. His handheld scanner beeped and whirred, casting pulses of soft light across the collapsed walls.

A voice called out from nearby, soft, smooth, like silk gliding over bare skin.

"Choktoo, did your scanners pick something up?"

He turned. A humanoid figure approached, her movements graceful, almost too fluid to be natural. Her voice carried the weight of both wonder and sorrow.

Choktoo opened his mandibles, clicking softly as he spoke.

"Yes. A fascinating find. Our scans indicate the entire civilization perished during a very short span of time. Simultaneously, in some regions. Biological signatures show three in the lower sections of the dwelling, likely a food preparation area, all deceased in the same room. Another body was found in the upper region. A small, enclosed space. Possibly a storage unit."

She nodded thoughtfully, the light from her scanner reflecting in her dark, glassy eyes.

"Our global sweep found similar conditions across the planet. The pattern repeats everywhere. According to their records, the species called themselves... Humans."

Choktoo stared at his device, antennae twitching.

"Do we know what caused this mass event? Why did they simply stop eating? Stop sleeping?"

She shook her head slowly.

"No. It doesn't make sense. The food is mere feet from where some of them died. Fully preserved. Untouched."

Choktoo paused, lowering his scanner.

"A civilization's existence snuffed out, and we may never know how or why."

She tilted her head.

"Curious."

And the wind whispered through the ruins, passing over bones, wires, and long-dead screens.

Choktoo reached down, brushing aside a layer of dust as he picked up one of the small devices. The screen blinked softly to life, displaying a logo: Veldt Inc.

His mandibles clicked thoughtfully.

"Perhaps collecting a few of these and analyzing them would prove useful?" he suggested, holding the device up to the dim light.

His female counterpart didn't respond immediately.

But she already held one in her hand.

Her eyes were glazed over slightly, pupils dilated as she stared at something on the screen, transfixed, silent.

Choktoo smiled to himself.

Yes. These artifacts would offer much to learn.

He looked forward to diving into the history, the culture, the stories.

To understanding these... Humans.

Six

The Hero I Married

The eggs crackled and popped next to the corned beef hash in the well-worn cast iron pan, releasing a mouthwatering aroma that seemed to wrap itself around the cozy kitchen like an invisible blanket. The mixture of sizzling grease, rich spices, and savory meat perfumed the air, promising a hearty breakfast and a moment of peace before the day carried them away again.

Anastasia moved with graceful urgency, the hem of her soft blue dress brushing against her calves as she turned and filled a ceramic mug with steaming coffee. She placed it precisely on the worn oak table, the slightest smile tugging at her lips.

Her dress whispered against her slender legs as she pivoted back to the stove. She scooped generous portions of eggs and hash onto a simple white plate, carefully arranging them with an instinctive, loving touch. No detail was too small when it came to Carter. Everything had to be perfect, or at least as perfect as she could make it for him.

She set the plate on the table with a satisfied nod, adjusting the silverware so it lined up just right. Her heart fluttered with familiar, almost girlish excitement as she heard his footsteps approach. Right on time.

Carter Stase. Her husband. The man who carried the weight of an entire city on his broad shoulders and still managed to smile at her like she was his whole world.

Carter stood like a man chiseled out of marble, every angle of his jawline sharp, like it had been carved with purpose by an artist who had no choice but to make perfection. His eyes were a deep, striking blue, like the calmest sky before a storm. The kind that could calm your nerves or send you spiraling into a wave of emotion with just one glance. His body was the epitome of strength, every muscle defined under the skin, but without the bulk of a bodybuilder. No, he was the perfect balance of power and agility, a form built for grace as much as might. His dark hair was slightly tousled, as if he had just come back from a battle, or maybe a stormy night on the balcony, contemplating the world. Every inch of him seemed to scream *hero*, yet there was a gentleness beneath his fierce exterior. A man who could lift the world on his shoulders and still make you feel like the only person in the room.

Anastasia leaned down, her dark hair brushing his cheek as she kissed him softly. Her eyes shimmered with undeniable passion, the kind that never faded no matter how many mornings they spent together. From the very first moment she met him, she had been utterly and irreversibly in love. He was her anchor, her champion, her everything.

"Good morning, dear," she murmured, her voice catching slightly as a blush colored her cheeks.

Carter's smile was the kind that could light up even the darkest corners of the world. He reached for her hand, squeezing it gently before speaking.

"Good morning, Anastasia. Did you sleep well?" he asked, his voice a familiar balm that soothed the invisible worries she always carried.

She laughed softly, almost shyly, as she dished up her own plate and placed it across from him. Her fingers brushed lightly over the rim of her coffee cup as she settled into her seat.

"How could I not after last night?" she said, casting him a playful glance from beneath her lashes.

Carter chuckled, the sound rich and low, and for a moment the heavy realities of the world beyond their walls disappeared.

"Will you be going out today?" The question tumbled from Anastasia's lips before she could stop it. Her fingers tightened briefly around her fork.

She hated asking and hated more the answer she knew was coming. Carter was not just a man to her. He was a symbol, a beacon. The shining hope of a city teetering constantly on the edge. Every time he left, a part of her could not help but wonder if he would return.

But she also knew better than anyone that power like his came with duty too heavy to ignore. And Carter Stase had never once turned away from it.

He nodded quietly. "Yes, I must, I'm sorry, my dear. Scar Tissue has been spotted in the city. I worry he may cause some problems."

Scar Tissue was a nightmare, a villain shrouded in mystery. No one knew his true appearance or his powers. All anyone knew was the trail of devastation he left behind: cities ransacked, lives destroyed, and victims who could remember nothing about him except how kind he seemed, right before everything went black. In his wake, survivors would sit in shock, covered in the blood of their loved ones, but unable to recall a single detail about the monster who had taken everything from them. He was dangerous. More than one hero had crossed paths with him, and each of them had suffered the same fate: they were unable to remember anything about their encounter.

Anastasia's heart tightened at the thought. She didn't like the idea of Carter, otherwise known as Everguard, the hero who meant everything to her, going after such a shadowy, dangerous foe. She sat quietly; her gaze fixed on her coffee. The dark liquid sat still in its cup, steam curling lazily from the top. Hers was decaf today. The first time she'd ever chosen it. She loved the caffeine, the warmth it gave her, the sharpness that came with each sip. But today, her thoughts were too heavy.

She wanted to tell him, to ask him to stay. Maybe sit this one out and let someone else handle Scar Tissue. But she couldn't, not yet anyway.

She longed to tell him about the pregnancy tests she'd taken. She had to. She wanted him to know. But this wasn't the time. He was about to face a danger that could take him from her, and she didn't want to distract him. Not when every part of her wanted to scream for him to stay, to promise he'd come back to her.

"Are you alright, dear?" Carter asked, looking up from his coffee cup at her with a hint of curiosity.

She blushed again and nodded quickly. "Yes, of course I am. I just worry for you."

Carter gave her his charming smile and stood, walking around the table. He bent down and kissed her forehead gently. In his deep voice he said, "Don't worry. Everything will be fine. Besides, I'm bringing backup today. Everything should go smoothly. Now then, I best be going or I'll miss the others. Thank you for breakfast, my dear."

Anastasia stood quickly, wrapping her arms around him in a tight hug before walking him to the door. One of the staff rushed over to clear the dishes. She could have had the staff cook them breakfast, but Anastasia preferred to take care of breakfast herself. She liked doing it for her husband. He deserved her attention, after all.

The two stepped out onto the porch, and Carter kissed her once more before dashing off into the sky. Anastasia folded her arms beneath her chest and watched him fly off, worry clouding her expression as he soared toward the city.

Turning back to look at their massive home, the home he had provided for them, she couldn't help but feel a deep sense of gratitude. They were both fortunate. The president had given them this place, paid them well, and showered them with fame for their efforts in keeping the city and country safe.

She traced her fingers along the doorframe, letting out a long, deep sigh. She hated this part. Waiting at home, wondering if he was alright.

Sighing again, she went inside and turned on the television, keeping it tuned to the news. She liked to have it on in case her husband made an appearance.

Her day passed much like any other. Her husband did not want her to work. He did not wish her to strain herself. That was why they had staff. Still, she found little things to do here and there, tasks she hoped he would not notice, just to keep herself busy.

When she was not watching a television show on her tablet or shopping, she was reading. This week's book was a new one, an intriguing story about a shapeshifting bard. Even as she read, she kept the television on, her eyes flickering toward it every few minutes in case she missed something important. So far, there had been nothing new.

One of the staff moved quietly beside her, washing the dishes and cleaning up the remains of her earlier cooking. Anastasia set her book down and made her way to the counter, placing her empty coffee mug down for the servant to collect.

Just then, the sharp sound of breaking news filled the room.

Spinning on her heels, Anastasia turned to face the television.

"Breaking news," the anchor announced, her voice tense as she began to speak. "At this very moment, we have reports that the supervillain known as Scar Tissue is robbing Sun City Bank. Multiple hostages are confirmed to be inside with him."

Anastasia's hand flew to her mouth as she stared at the screen in horror.

The anchor continued, her voice growing more urgent. "Just in, it seems Everguard has arrived along with Silver Tempest. Officers on the scene are telling us to back away. We are attempting to get a video feed from inside the bank."

The footage cut into a shaky video showing Everguard phasing through a wall into the bank. A moment later, Silver

Tempest appeared, waving his hand. A brilliant beam of light sliced through the metal bars covering a nearby window, forcing it open.

Anastasia stood frozen, her heart pounding as she watched the scene unfold.

The crowd gathered behind the barricades, straining for a glimpse of the battle raging inside the Sun City Bank.

At first, there was only tense silence, broken by the low murmur of the reporters speaking into their microphones. Then it came, sudden and jarring, a thunderous crash that made the ground tremble beneath their feet.

Gasps rippled among the bystanders as the walls of the bank seemed to shudder. Muffled booms echoed from within, sharp cracks of gunfire or something worse. Windows rattled in their frames. A deep metallic groan vibrated the air, and was followed by the unmistakable sound of something heavy slamming into the marble interior.

People clutched one another as a series of ear-splitting explosions rocked the building. Sparks erupted from behind the thick stone facade.

But nobody could see what was happening inside.

Only the terrible noises told the story.

Another violent crash sent a spider web of cracks crawling up the bank's front windows. Then, with a sound like the earth itself splitting, a body was hurled through the air.

Silver Tempest burst through a second-story window, the glass exploding around him in a thousand glittering shards. He flew through the open air in a limp, graceless arc. His body was soaked in blood, red staining his silver costume until it was almost unrecognizable.

He hit the ground hard with a sickening thud that echoed down the block.

The crowd screamed.

As the horrified onlookers backed away, a heavy, wet sound followed. Anastasia, frozen at her television, watched in horror as something else dropped from the broken window above.

A heart.

It hit the pavement with a dull, revolting splatter, landing just inches from Silver Tempest's mangled body.

The reporters stumbled backward. Officers rushed forward, their guns raised, shouting orders to retreat. Sirens began to wail in the distance.

Anastasia's hands trembled as she covered her mouth, her eyes wide with terror. Somewhere deep inside, a cold, nauseating dread took root. She knew Carter was still in there. Alone.

The world seemed to freeze as Anastasia watched in horror. Inside the shattered bank building, the battle raged on. Through the thick cloud of dust and debris, two silhouettes clashed like titans, but it was impossible to make out who was gaining the upper hand. Each brutal impact shook the air, every shuddering crash and splintering of walls causing the crowd outside to flinch.

Screams echoed from within. Terrified cries rose and fell as hostages either fought to survive or feared their final moments. Glass exploded outward, raining onto the sidewalks. The sirens wailed like some tortured beast in the background, but no one dared move. All anyone could do was watch and pray.

Then, suddenly, the thick cloud cover above the city cracked open. A radiant figure descended from the heavens. Light pooled around his form as he touched down, the sheer force of his landing cracking the pavement beneath his boots. Broad shoulders, a sculpted frame like something out of myth, and a golden aura that shimmered against the gloom.

The reporter's voice broke through the chaos, shaky but electrified with hope.

"Folks, we are very fortunate. Solarius is here to lend a hand!"

Gasps and cheers rippled through the stunned crowd. Anastasia clasped her hands tightly together against her chest, hardly daring to breathe. Solarius raised one glowing hand, his fingers spreading wide, targeting one of the battling figures inside the bank.

Anastasia's heart nearly stopped. Was he aiming at the right one?

In a blinding instant, a concentrated beam of pure solar energy blasted from his palm. The light carved through the chaos, slamming into one of the figures. The victim was engulfed in a searing flash, their body breaking apart like brittle ash caught in a firestorm. Bones crumbled to dust, scattering across the floor of the bank.

For a heartbeat, there was silence.

Then, one by one, the people around the bank collapsed. Anastasia stumbled back and fell hard onto the cold tile. Her eyes were wide, her breath rasping in her throat. On the screen, the crowd was dropping as if some unseen force had stolen their strength. Even Solarius staggered, clutching his head in both hands, his golden aura flickering dangerously.

Anastasia gasped, struggling against the crushing weight pressing against her mind. Something was wrong.

As she fought for air, her memories began flooding back. Not the neat, orderly memories she had always known. True memories. Darker, raw, things she was never supposed to remember.

Things someone had taken from her, replacing them with *perfect* memories.

She looked down at her shaking hands, then back up at the television screen.

Her husband was gone.

The truth began to invade her mind. She was beginning to remember. Pieces that had never quite fit before snapped into a picture so horrifying, she could hardly breathe.

He had never existed.

At least, not in the way she had believed. Everguard existed only in everyone's minds.

A sob ripped from her throat. She pressed a trembling hand to her mouth, her tears falling freely now. The man she had loved, trusted, who had kissed her forehead and promised her everything, he was Scar Tissue. The whole time. The villain and monster.

His power was to make people see what he wanted them to see. There was no mansion or staff. She stood in a small kitchen. In a tiny run-down home. It was all an illusion.

Anastasia collapsed onto all fours, her hair falling into her face as she wept against the cold, uncaring floor.

He had tricked everyone. Sure, he had tricked her, but he had given her that perfect place, happiness, and now it was gone. It had ceased to exist. Even though it had only ever existed in her mind.

She looked down at her stomach.

Now she was carrying Scar Tissue's child.

Terror and sorrow twisted inside her like jagged glass. She lifted her tear-streaked face toward the television again. The cameras captured the chaos as the crowd outside the bank remembered. Horrified screams filled the air. People clutched their heads, wailed, and crumbled to the ground. They remembered watching their loved ones die at Scar Tissue's hands. They remembered his pale, scarred face, the radiation burns marking him like a cruel brand.

And they remembered how they had been forced to love him.

Anastasia stayed where she was, broken and small against the vinal floor.

Was her love for him ever real?

Or had it been just another lie, planted in her heart like a seed that had grown into this living tree she called love?

She didn't have an answer to that. In fact, she may never have an answer to it.

But one thing she did know. She would not waste the life growing inside her. She would not let the sins of the father define the future of the child. She refused to raise this child, not in the shadow of Scar Tissue, but in the light Carter had pretended to offer. She would raise him to be better. To be true.

The child would be magnificent.

Sobbing, but resolute, Anastasia gathered herself. She packed quickly; her movements frantic but determined. A few essentials, some memories that were hers alone. Then, without looking back, she slipped out the door, her heart hammering in her chest.

She prayed no one would recognize her.

And somewhere deep inside her shattered soul, a flicker of hope survived. Maybe her child would have Scar Tissue's powers. Maybe this child could give her that world of happiness she had lost.

SEVEN

THE DAY I LET HER LIVE

Arthur Tanner III was in his glory.

Today was a big day, *the* big day. He was about to marry the love of his life, the radiant, ever-gushing Maria Elestonza.

She was still asleep, lying in bed. Arthur stood there for a moment, soaking it in. Today everything would change.

With a grin tugging at his lips, Arthur ran a hand through his hair and pulled himself upright. He scratched absentmindedly at his wrist and let out a yawn, then staggered toward the coffee maker like a man on a mission, or at least a man in desperate need of caffeine.

There was a lot to do. Tuxedos, vows, rings, guests. He wasn't complaining. Hell, no. He was buzzing with excitement.

He reached for the coffee maker switch, but his hand froze mid-air. Something caught his eye.

Light. Faint, but unmistakable, glowing softly from his wrist.

Confused, he turned his arm and squinted. There, shimmering just beneath the skin, was a number.

His first thought? Maybe one of those trendy glow-in-the-dark tattoos people got after a few too many drinks. Wouldn't be the first time he'd done something stupid during a night out.

He chuckled to himself, until he realized...

He didn't remember getting any tattoos.

And this number?

It was changing.

But then he noticed something else.

The number was counting down.

Arthur froze.

He stared at the digits, transfixed, and then reached up to touch them. His fingers pressed against his wrist, expecting... *something*. A bump or a chip, maybe even a device under the skin.

But no. Just flesh.

Warm, normal, human flesh.

The number continued to tick downward, unwavering and uncaring what he thought of it.

20:46:32

20:46:31

20:46:30

Arthur's stomach churned. What's all this about, then?

He'd never seen anything like it. Part of him wanted to claw at the skin, to tear the glowing numbers out with his bare hands. Something primal inside him recoiled from it, like it wasn't supposed to be there. Like it didn't *belong* to him.

Maybe it was some weird countdown to the wedding? He wouldn't put it past his groomsman to prank him with some custom app synced to his smartwatch. Telling him his freedom ended in so many hours.

No, he wasn't wearing any smartwatch.

Also, he did the math in his head. None of it made a bit of sense.

The wedding was at five.

That was just over eleven hours away.

This countdown?

The number was over twenty.

Tilting his head, Arthur stepped into the restroom, curiosity giving way to growing concern. He grabbed a bar of soap and a washcloth, then began scrubbing his wrist like a man trying to erase sin itself.

But the numbers remained.

They counted down, glowing as if to mock him and his efforts.

A bead of sweat slid down his temple. Anxiety was blooming fast, coiling in his gut like something alive.

He had to talk to someone.

Tyga.

His best man. His best friend since childhood. If anyone had answers, or at least a smartass theory, it'd be him.

Arthur cast one last glance across the room at his beautiful bride-to-be, still peacefully sleeping. He sighed, heart thudding, and bolted for the door.

He raced down the hall and pounded on Tyga's door with his fist like it owed him money.

"Tyga! Hey, mate! Let me in, I gotta show you something!"

A few long seconds later, the door creaked open.

Tyga stood there, shirtless, hair pointing in twelve directions, and looking like he'd lost a bar fight with his own liver.

"Oi, mate, pack it in, yeah?" he groaned, wincing at the light. "Me 'ead's poundin' like a drumline in a meat grinder. You tryna kill me, or what?"

"Listen, mate, I'm sorry," Arthur said, eyes wide and uneasy. "But something's happened."

Tyga squinted at him, then glanced back over his shoulder at the lump under the sheets in his room. Grabbing a shirt and beginning to put it on. He stepped out and gently pulled the door shut behind him.

"One o' the bridesmaids, yeah?" he said with a cheeky grin. "Didn't catch her name, but she had them eyes wot'd make ya melt, she did. Now... what's got your knickers in a twist?"

Arthur held up his arm, palm up, showing Tyga the glowing numbers ticking away on his wrist.

"You ever seen anything like this?" he asked.

Tyga blinked, then grabbed Arthur's arm and held it up to the light, frowning.

"What's it countin' down to, then?"

"I don't know, Tyga," Arthur snapped, voice low and urgent. "That's why I'm *here*, talking to you."

Tyga scratched the back of his neck, staring at the numbers like they might start doing tricks.

"Well, bloody hell," he muttered. "You always gotta pick the weirdest days to go fallin' into sci-fi shite."

"What d'you mean?" Arthur snapped. "I had nothin' to do with this, I just *woke up* with it."

Tyga smirked, clearly enjoying himself way too much for someone still half-pickled.

"Did ya talk to Maria yet? Maybe she 'ad it done to keep ya honest, yeah? Bit o' pre-weddin' insurance, make sure ya don't go wanderin'."

Arthur blinked. That hadn't even crossed his mind.

Maybe... Maria did this?

No. No way. She wanted everything *perfect*. The woman nearly had a meltdown when the seating chart got printed in the wrong font. A glowin' countdown on her fiancé? She'd go full Bridezilla and burn the venue to the ground.

"Nah," Arthur muttered. "That don't add up. If I got a wrinkle in me suit, she's throwin' a fit. This? This ain't somethin' she'd be alright with."

Tyga tilted his head and scratched his scruffy chin. "Yeah... you might be right there, mate."

He rubbed his temples with both hands like he was trying to squeeze his brain into working. "Tell ya what, let's get a bit o' hair o' the dog, yeah? Maybe once me skull stops poundin', I can actually *think*."

He gave Arthur's wrist another look. "So what's it countin' down to then? Ceremony?"

Arthur shook his head. "No. It's later. After the wedding."

Tyga elbowed him and grinned. "Maybe it's countin' down to the ol' *wedding night action*, eh? Bit o' the honeymoon horizontal hokey-pokey?"

Arthur shot him a glare. "Can you *please* be serious, Tyga?"

Tyga backed off, hands raised. "Alright, alright! Just havin' a laugh. You've got a glowy countdown on yer arm, I've got goblins dancin' in me skull, bloody strange mornin' all around, innit?"

"Yeah, it is, Tyga," Arthur muttered. "Let's get to the pub. Maybe we can figure this out over a pint."

The two made their way down the hall toward the pub, their footsteps echoing off the quiet corridor.

Tyga shoved his hands into his pockets. "You reckon it's the end of the world or somethin'?"

Arthur glanced at his wrist, the glowing countdown ticking away like a silent warning.

"Oh yeah," he said dryly. "And the powers that be thought, 'Let's give the fate of the world to *this* guy. A bloke with a credit score under 600 and no upper body strength.' Seems real likely."

Tyga laughed. "Oi, don't sell yourself short, mate. You pulled Maria, didn't ya? Still don't know how you managed *that* one."

Arthur chuckled, because honestly, neither did he.

But whatever it was the universe liked about him, he had to keep doing it.

The pub doors creaked open, and the familiar warmth hit them like a blanket soaked in spilled beer and cheap cologne. A decent crowd was already inside, some nursing hangovers, others clearly working up to fresh ones.

Arthur and Tyga slid onto bar stools like they owned the place. The bartender, a woman with messy curls and a wicked grin, sauntered over with two pints already in hand.

"'Ello, boys," she said, voice smooth and raspy. "You look like you're nursin' a right proper headache."

Tyga winked. "Oi, Birdie, I reckon you were tryin' to snog me last night."

Birdie smirked, resting her elbows on the bar. "Maybe I was, Tyga. Maybe you needed it."

Arthur raised his pint, cutting in. "Alright, Tyga, enough flirtin'. Can you help me out here or what?"

"Yeah, yeah, I gotcha," Tyga said, finally dragging his eyes off Birdie's backside with the grace of a man who absolutely did not care about being subtle.

"Right, so... after the pub last night, you staggered off 'ome, I went up with that bridesmaid, bit of a wild one, she was, left teeth marks on me shoulder, and you carried on with Maria, yeah? Anythin' funny happen between droppin' us off and gettin' through yer door?"

Arthur frowned, digging through the fog in his head.

"I think... we just went in and passed out," he said slowly. "She was nearly as sozzled as I was. We barely made it to the bed."

Tyga narrowed his eyes. "So nothin' odd? No blokes lurkin' in the wardrobe? No shady types slappin' glowin' tattoos on ya in the middle of the night?"

Arthur shook his head. "No. I don't remember anything but falling asleep."

Then his brow creased. A flicker of paranoia crept in.

"You don't think someone broke in, do you? Like... a staff member or something?"

Birdie spun around, eyes sharp as ever. "Oi, what was up with Maria's old man last night?"

Tyga chimed in, "Yeah, mate, what was all that about? He went proper mad, didn't he?"

Arthur tried to scrape the fog from his memory. He did recall Maria's father shouting, loud enough to wake the dead.

Something about Arthur's own dad owing money. Or some business gone sour.

"I dunno, mate. He's usually pretty laid back, yeah?" Arthur said.

Tyga shook his head. "Not last night. Nah, he was fumin'. Wonder what set him off."

Arthur frowned, thinking it through. "Maria's told me he's got a hot 'ead sometimes. Never seen it till last night. She said it's best to just agree with 'im, he can be dangerous when riled."

Tyga scratched his head, squinting.

"You reckon he's part of some mafia or summat? That sounded like proper mafia talk to me."

Arthur frowned, chewing it over. Truth was, he hadn't spent much time with Maria's father. The man always seemed quiet, kept to himself. Withdrawn. Maria once told him her dad was all about his business, and that you'd best not stand between him and it... or there'd be hell to pay. Arthur never did ask what she meant by that.

Didn't feel like his place.

All he'd cared about was that Maria, this beautiful, brilliant woman who by all reason was way out of his league, was actually with him.

Tyga laughed, shaking his head. "Dangerous? Pfft. Nothin' a good scrap can't fix, I'm sure."

Arthur cracked a grin. "Oi, remember that scrap we 'ad down in Bethnal Green, yeah?"

Tyga's grin widened. "We got proper rat-arsed after that, didn't we?"

"Oi, we need to get movin'. Gotta pick up our tux and try 'em on for the ceremony," Arthur said, glancing at his watch.

"Yeah, mate, Maria'll kill us if those don't fit. Thanks for the drink, Birdie. We'll talk about that snog later!" he added with a grin.

Birdie turned, eyes sparkling with mischief. "Oi! You lot think you can just pop in here anytime for a snog, do ya? Might have to start charging for the pleasure, you know."

Tyga laughed. "Charge away, Birdie. Might be the only way to keep you in line."

Birdie smirked. "Keep me in line? Mate, I'm the only one around here who knows how to handle you two clowns."

Arthur shook his head, grinning. "She's got a point there."

The two made their way down the street toward the tux shop. The sign hung behind the glass door was still wobbling from the shopkeeper flipping it; looked like the place had just opened.

Inside, Arthur looked around, still half in disbelief that he was here at all.

The shopkeeper, a large woman with a no-nonsense glare, greeted them. "Oi, what'll it be?"

"Eh, two tuxedos for the Tanner party?" Arthur said.

She checked her paperwork and pulled two tuxedos from the rack, handing them over. "Try 'em on in the side room, will ya?" she said as they headed to the fitting rooms.

Arthur was the first to step out of the changing room.

He tugged at the lapels, gave the tie a quick pat, and turned to face the mirror.

It was the first time he'd ever seen himself in a suit, at least a *proper* suit, and to his surprise, he rather liked what he saw.

He turned side to side, checking every angle like he was trying to catch himself off guard.

No, he wasn't some posh tuxedo expert, but still... the fit was sharp, the shoulders crisp, and for once, he actually looked the part.

Dashing, even.

Tyga stepped out next, shifting his weight from one foot to the other like he was auditioning for the cover of *GQ*.

He popped the collar, let the tie dangle loose like it was part of the look, and struck a pose as if the shop floor was his personal runway.

"Can't say I look too shabby," he said with a smirk, smoothing his lapel. "At this rate, I might bag all of Maria's bridesmaids."

Arthur rolled his eyes, arms crossed. "You look like someone let a rock star loose in a tux shop."

Tyga grinned wider. "Exactly."

Arthur checked his watch again, heart giving a subtle jump. Time was flying, and the ceremony was fast approaching. "We've gotta leg it," he muttered. Tuxedo bags in hand and nerves setting in, the two dashed back to the pub. They paused just long enough to grab a quick pint, half tradition, half survival, downed them in a single pull, and turned toward the door.

Birdie leaned on the bar with a grin. "Oi, don't go spillin' anything on those suits, yeah? You boys clean up too nice to ruin it now."

Arthur flashed a crooked smile. "You're a legend, Birdie."

Tyga gave a wink and blew her a sloppy kiss. "Save me a snog for later, sweetheart."

With a final wave, they were off.

For the first time that morning, Arthur's thoughts drifted away from the glowing numbers on his wrist. The wedding had taken hold of his attention like a tide swallowing sand. And why not? Everything felt perfect.

The ceremony itself was flawless. Vows were spoken with trembling voices and bright eyes. Arthur felt a lump in his throat as Maria said his name, her hands warm in his. They kissed to a round of cheers, and Arthur, grinning like a fool, literally swept her off her feet and carried her down the chapel steps. Guests tossed petals and shouted their blessings as the couple made their way to the hall, ready to celebrate until their legs gave out.

The reception was alive with music and laughter. Tables groaned under the weight of roasted meats, pastries, and open bottles. Arthur and Maria couldn't stop smiling, couldn't stop touching, whispering between kisses, laughter shared over full glasses. She looked radiant, cheeks flushed pink from dancing and wine. Every time he leaned in, she blushed like it was the first time he'd ever spoken her name.

Tyga, meanwhile, was a menace of pure charisma. More sozzled than he'd been the night before, he danced with every bridesmaid who'd let him, possibly some twice, and made sure they all knew his name, even if he wouldn't remember theirs come morning.

It was the kind of night that felt like the beginning of something permanent. A perfect snapshot. A high note that Arthur never wanted to come down from.

The group had long since lost track of time. Laughter turned to slurred singing, dancing to stumbling, and now, well into the night, some guests sat slack-jawed at their tables, blinking around the room like they couldn't quite remember where they were or how they got there.

But over the hum of celebration, a sharp burst of words rang out, louder than the music.

Arthur turned his head just in time to see Maria's father and his own locked in a heated argument near the head table, faces red, voices raised, teeth bared like dogs about to bite.

He rose slowly, a tight knot forming in his gut. The last thing he wanted was a scene. Maria, glassy-eyed from drink but sharp with sudden dread, reached up and caught his hand.

"Please... no," she whispered, her voice trembling.

Arthur gave her a soft smile. "It's alright, my love. I'll just calm them down, yeah? I'm sure it's just a misunderstanding."

He stepped away from her and moved through the crowd, weaving past spinning dancers and drunk bridesmaids leaning on each other for balance.

The two men were chest to chest now, fists clenched at their sides like a dam about to break.

"Whoa, come on," Arthur said, placing himself between them, "let's not ruin Maria's big day, yeah?"

His father looked at him, eyes bloodshot, face taut with shame, and opened his mouth as if to explain. But before a word left his lips...

CRACK!

Maria's father drove a fist into the side of Arthur's father's jaw, snapping his head to the side with a sickening thud.

There was a beat. A silence. A breath.

Then his father came roaring back, throwing a wild punch that caught Maria's father clean across the mouth, splitting his lip and spraying blood onto the pristine white tablecloths nearby.

The fight exploded.

They lunged at each other like bulls, hands grabbing at shirts, fists hammering ribs and jaws, feet stumbling over chairs.

One blow sent Maria's father reeling backward into a long banquet table, candles toppled over, joined by cutlery as they clattered to the floor, a small flame sparked on a satin table runner.

No one noticed. Not yet.

Arthur shouted, trying to pull them apart, but the two men were locked in a savage tangle. His father tackled the other man into a pile of empty chairs, sending them skidding across the floor in a crash of metal and splinters.

Maria's father twisted, landed a punch to the gut, then surged forward, slamming his shoulder into Arthur's father and sending them both crashing onto another table. More candles fell, one landing in a puddle of spilled wine, another into a paper flower centerpiece. Flames flickered to life.

Gasps spread through the room.

Someone screamed.

The party was no longer a celebration, it had unraveled, and fast.

Tyga rushed forward, shoving chairs and half-toppled tables aside to reach Arthur through the thickening smoke. The flames were spreading fast now, licking up curtains, devouring decorations, and filling the air with choking blackness.

"Arthur!" he called out, coughing. "We gotta shut this down!"

The two fathers were still going at it, bloodied, gasping, shoving each other into wreckage like rabid dogs. Plates shattered underfoot. Arthur's father grabbed a bottle off a nearby table and swung it like a club, missing by inches.

Arthur tried again to pull them apart, but the heat was unbearable. Smoke clawed at his throat. Then, out of the corner of his eye, he saw someone sprint past, arms flailing, *engulfed in flame.*

A shriek echoed through the hall as the guest stumbled into a wall, crashing into a candelabra before vanishing into the blaze. The reality of the inferno crashed down on him like a weight.

The fire was no longer just spreading, it was consuming.

"Arthur! Grab Maria, mate! We gotta leg it, *now!*" Tyga bellowed, his voice hoarse from smoke.

But the moment shattered.

With a groan like thunder, one of the wooden pillars, half-burnt through, collapsed from the ceiling and came crashing down.

It struck Tyga across the head with a sickening *crack.*

"No, Tyga!" Arthur screamed.

He dove to the floor beside him, heart racing, eyes wide. Tyga's body was limp, twisted at an angle that felt wrong. Arthur reached for his neck, nothing. No beat. No breath. Just... stillness.

Arthur's scream ripped through the roaring fire.

Gritting his teeth, tears cutting streaks through the soot on his face, he forced himself up and stumbled toward the table where he had last seen his bride. He scanned the smoke-blurred chaos. Where was she?

Then, he spotted her.

Maria was backed into a corner, surrounded by flames. Her eyes were wide with terror, and her gown, white, beautiful, and full of delicate lace, was already beginning to catch.

"No!" Arthur shouted, charging forward.

She struggled with the dress, trying to rip it free, to tear the fabric away from her skin, but the fire moved faster. The frills ignited, flames racing up her body like they'd been waiting for her all along.

She screamed, a raw, gut-wrenching sound of pain and fear, as the fire overtook her.

Arthur was too late. Too slow. Again.

He dropped to his knees and let out a howl of grief, a sound no human should ever have to make. All around him, the world burned. The air shimmered with heat. The walls groaned as if the building itself was weeping.

And then, he saw it.

A flicker on his wrist.

Blinking.

He looked down.

00:00:00

And just beneath it, two small circles of light:

[Reset] [Accept]

A pulse of memory struck him like lightning. Images, flashes, fragments of pain. Maria burning. Tyga dying. Over and over.

He'd been here before.

Dozens of times? Hundreds?

How many times had he failed?

How many times had he pressed *Reset*?

The flames were closing in now, dancing at his boots. Heat pressed into his skin, demanding his choice.

Arthur stared at Maria's still-burning body through the smoke. His soul cracked open. He couldn't let this be the end.

His finger hovered... then pressed down on *Reset*.

The world screamed.

It twisted. Shattered. Collapsed.

Everything around him fell away like ash in the wind, and then, just as the pain of it all became too much...

...a blinding white light engulfed his vision.

Arthur blinked, the world reassembling around him in a blur of color and light. His vision cleared, revealing a silhouette standing above him.

Maria.

She smiled down at him, radiant and familiar. "First time?" she asked, a playful giggle dancing in her voice.

His heart clenched. That voice. That smile.

He remembered this moment, the day they met.

Arthur sat up slowly, his limbs aching as if the echo of fire still lingered in his bones.

"Oh, careful," she said, offering a hand. "You had quite the tumble."

He took it, letting her pull him to his feet. His legs felt unsteady, the rollerblades laced tightly to his feet. He glanced down at them, then back at her, smiling faintly.

"Oh, I'll be alright," he said, the words leaving his mouth on reflex. He'd said them before. Too many times. Far too many.

He scanned the rink. He remembered the bright lights, and music playing from the old speakers. The scent of popcorn and cheap nachos filled the air. Off to the side, Tyga lounged on a bench with a girl straddling his lap, grinning like he'd just won the lottery. He threw Arthur a thumbs-up.

It felt like a dream. A cruel, beautiful dream.

Arthur turned back to Maria. She was smiling, like she always did, like nothing in the world could touch her. That smile... it had destroyed him, saved him, broken him, and healed him in loop after loop.

He loved her more than anything. With every ounce of his soul. But...

At what cost?

He stared into her eyes, the weight of the many lives he had seen with her pressing on his chest. How many resets had he tried? How many times had he clawed at fate to save her? To save Tyga? To make it all right?

All but one path.

He nodded to her softly, emotion tightening his throat. "Thank you," he whispered.

Maria tilted her head slightly, puzzled, but still smiling.

Arthur turned and skated away.

She watched him go, confusion blooming into something sadder. Her smile wavered, her eyes darkening with the hint of something lost. She didn't chase him. She just watched.

Arthur glided across the rink to where Tyga was laughing with his arm around the girl.

Tyga looked up as Arthur stopped. "Oi, mate. Ya blind? That one had eyes for you," he said with a smirk, nodding toward Maria.

Arthur shook his head, eyes rimmed with quiet pain. "Nah," he said softly. "I'm just headin' home. Not feelin' it anymore."

Tyga gave him a strange look, but didn't press.

Arthur turned, skated toward the exit. A single tear broke loose and rolled down his cheek. He didn't wipe it away. It was a symbol of his broken heart.

Outside, the wind was cool on his wet cheek.

He would never feel that love again. Not the way he had. Not the way she had given it.

But Maria was alive. Tyga was alive.

And for that... he would trade everything. Even his own happiness.

Eight

Delete me, I Dare You

[The Writer]

The birds... the majestic birds.

A hawk soared overhead, its shadow gliding over the couple stretched out beneath the day's brilliant sun.

Stan paused, pencil suspended mid-air. Slowly, he lowered it and stared down at the page.

Being an author was harder than people assumed: not just writing well, but *writing at all.*

No one reads to feel anymore, he thought bitterly. *They only read to dissect, dissect, dissect.*

Why is this happening in the story but not that?

Why can't he speak the language if he's from here?

What happened to the barn cat?

Why couldn't they just let a story *breathe?*

Life wasn't perfect. Neither was his story. And it didn't need to be.

It had started as a simple tale, Mark, a weary farmer, taking in his troubled niece. But somewhere along the way, the narrative began to bleed at the seams. Too many inconsistencies. Too many loose threads straying from the loom.

Now he found himself writing about James.

A side character. Unimportant by every standard... except to Stan.

He couldn't explain it, not even to himself, but something in him *needed* James to be perfect. Not just crafted, *real*.

Stan sighed.

James had appeared in the story *once*. One paragraph. Not even a line of dialogue. Just a mention in passing, and yet Stan couldn't stop thinking about him.

He flipped the pencil in his hand and erased a line.

James does not need a dog, he thought firmly. *No more dog for James.*

He scratched his head, annoyed at himself.

"Alright, back to the main character," he muttered.

Arn. The old farmer.

Stan's pencil hovered over the paper, unwilling to touch it.

Wait... why did Arn bring his niece here again?

Because she got into trouble, right?

What kind of trouble?

Stan stared at the page, frowning. The idea had been clear once, simple, even. But now it felt like trying to remember a dream while he was just waking up, staring into the morning light.

[The Character]

James sighed contentedly. Life wasn't half bad these days. He had a fiancée he adored, a beautiful home with a white picket fence, and a steady job at the local bar. It wasn't flashy, but it was *his*, and honestly? Things could've been a whole lot worse.

He stood on his front porch in the morning sunlight, a steaming mug of coffee in hand. His eyes drifted closed as the warmth kissed his face.

Now... where was his paper?

He looked around curiously. That was odd. Tot had usually brought it to him by now.

"Tot? Where are you, girl?" he called, scanning the yard.

No jingle of tags. No scratching at the door. No excited bark.

His best friend, Darryl, wandered up the front path, hands in his pockets.

"Hey, James. You lose something?" he asked.

"Yeah. Tot. My dog. She usually brings the paper."

Darryl blinked, then chuckled. "Your dog? You don't have a dog, James."

James paused.

A long silence hung between them.

Yes, he did. He *remembered* petting her. Her warm fur. Telling her she was a good girl. She slept at the foot of the bed every night, didn't she?

Darryl raised an eyebrow. "You got something extra in that coffee this morning?"

James forced a smile. "Clair must've slipped me some of the *good* stuff, huh?"

Darryl laughed and wandered off, but James just stood there, still as stone.

Mug in hand. Sunshine on his skin.

No dog.

But he knew, he *knew*, Tot existed. Somewhere.

He stepped inside, the scent of breakfast greeting him like an old friend. Clair was at the stove, humming softly as she flipped eggs in the pan.

James walked up behind her and kissed her cheek.

"Good morning, beautiful," he said with a grin. "How'd you sleep?"

Clair turned with a smile and kissed him back, this time on the lips, one leg lifting playfully, like they were in a movie.

"After last night? How could I not?" she purred.

James chuckled, basking in the glow of their little morning ritual. He pulled out a chair and sat down as she slid a plate of eggs in front of him.

"Hey," he said casually, "I haven't been able to find Tot. You know where she is?"

Clair paused, a crease forming between her brows.

"Tot?" she repeated, confused.

James raised an eyebrow. Maybe she didn't hear him right.

"Yeah. Small dog? Cute as can be?"

Clair laughed, brushing a strand of hair behind her ear.

"Is this your way of saying you want to get a dog?"

James froze. Just for a second. His smile faltered, but he masked it quickly.

They had walked Tot last night. Together. He *remembered* it. Her leash, her yappy bark, Clair laughing when Tot tried to chase a squirrel.

What's going on?

He opened the newspaper and stared at the front page, pretending to read. Something about a vote for a new baseball field. An author coming to town. Big headlines, but his eyes skimmed past them.

He wasn't reading. Not really.

All he could think about was Tot.

And how no one else seemed to remember she existed.

[The Writer]

Drugs.

Yeah, he was pretty sure Arn's niece had been into something, maybe pills, maybe worse. She went to meet her dealer, and that was when she witnessed it.

A murder.

Yes. That tracked.

Now she was being sent away to live with Arn. The family didn't know what else to do with her.

Okay. This was starting to come together.

Arn was a lonely old man working his farm by himself. Stubborn as a mule, pretending he didn't need anyone, but he'd be happy for the company. He just wouldn't admit it.

Stan paused, pencil hovering over the page.

His thoughts drifted again.

James.

What was James doing right now?

He stared down at the notebook, frowning. Why was he so obsessed with that character? It didn't make any sense. James had barely even *been* in the story.

One paragraph. No dialogue. Just a name, a shadow on the wall.

And yet... Stan couldn't let him go.

Maybe James was at the store.

Yeah, that made sense. He'd gone to the local market to grab a few things. Something simple. Something grounded.

The cashier was chatty, as usual. She brought up Arn's situation, how the niece was staying with him now, poor girl. Said she'd heard it was because of some kind of incident, but no one was talking specifics.

Stan jotted it down in his notebook, pencil moving almost on autopilot. He wasn't sure if he was writing what he wanted... or what he was *hearing*.

Then something new slipped in.

The cashier mentioned an author.

Some big-shot writer was in town.

James blinked.

An author?

He did enjoy a good read. Maybe he'd stop by.

Stan tilted his head and scribbled into the margin:

"Goes to meet the author. Picks up his book."

Okay. Now we're getting somewhere.

[The Character]

James arrived at the book signing, the new title tucked under his arm.

The cover was odd.

An old farmer stood beside a teenager with neon-colored hair and a chain through their lip. Behind them stretched a crowd of townsfolk, some generic, others strangely familiar.

There was a gas station attendant who looked exactly like Pete, right down to the oil-stained cap and that ever-present tooth-whistle smirk. A woman clutched a tray of vegetables like she was posing for a grocery store flyer, and for a moment James swore it was Mrs. Klein, right down to the mole on her cheek.

But then there was the couple.

They were tucked near the center, caught mid-laugh. The man was taller, with a half-smile and short brown hair. The woman had shoulder-length auburn curls, her head resting on his chest, eyes closed like she trusted him with the world.

James tilted the book slightly, frowning.

Something about her seemed familiar, like a faded photograph he'd seen once in someone else's scrapbook. The man looked... maybe like him? But not enough. His hair was too full, and the jaw too sharp. It could've been coincidence. Or an artist's placeholder. But Clair, yeah, she looked a little too close.

He gave a soft snort and shook it off. Towns like his didn't get famous authors, and they definitely didn't get painted onto book covers.

The title read: *How I Changed My Life.*

He wasn't sure it was really his thing.

Aside from the weird moment earlier, forgetting he didn't have a dog, or dreaming that he did, his life was just about perfect. Probably just a vivid dream, he figured. Nothing worth obsessing over.

He stepped up to the table where the author sat. The man reached out and took the book, flipping it open to the title page. Without looking up, he signed his name.

James watched him closely.

There was something... familiar about the guy. He couldn't quite place it, but it made his skin itch.

Another person stepped forward, engaging the author in excited conversation. James waited patiently, watching as the man chewed absently on a pencil, deep in thought while answering a question.

Then, without realizing, the author turned back to James and said, "Oh! Terribly sorry."

He handed the book, and the pencil, to James without even noticing.

James blinked at the pencil. Before he could say anything, the author was already mid-sentence with the next fan, completely absorbed.

James hesitated. He considered tossing the pencil in the nearest trash bin. But something stopped him.

What if this guy's more famous than I thought?

That pencil could be worth something one day.

He slipped it into his pocket and headed home.

In truth, James had no idea who the author was.

He lived in a small town, and little ever happened, certainly no one famous would drop in. Honestly, the whole town had gone into a tizzy over something as simple as old Arn's niece coming to visit.

That alone should tell you how quiet things usually were.

He opened his car door and strolled up the walkway to his house. Pushing the door open, he called out, "Clair, I'm home!"

He set the book on the dinner table just as Clair came bouncing down the stairs.

She leaned in and kissed him. "Hello, hun," she said, beaming.

James smiled and wrapped his arms around her, pulling her into a deeper kiss.

"Hey, babe. What've you been up to all day?"

She grinned, moving into the kitchen to start prepping dinner.

"Oh, nothing much. Just finishing up some chores around the house."

James glanced around the living room. Everything looked neat. Peaceful.

"Well, the place looks great."

She blushed, waving him off. "You're just saying that."

After a pause, she asked, "So... how was your day? Anything interesting?"

He shook his head. "Not really. Some famous author was in town today, so I picked up a book. Not sure it's my thing, but hey, gotta support the smaller guys, right?"

She giggled. "Yes, I suppose you're right."

She didn't bother to look at the book, too busy trying to get dinner on the table. They chatted as they always did, talking about their days and making plans for the weekend.

The night passed peacefully.

Dinner.

Laughter.

Warm touches and soft smiles.

Eventually, they climbed into bed and fell asleep in each other's arms.

James couldn't have been happier.

His life was perfect.

[The Writer]

Stan sat hunched at his cluttered desk, the lined yellow notepad balanced just so beneath his forearm. Pencil between his fingers, well-worn eraser smudged and blunted, he stared down at the names he'd so carefully scribbled in blocky, all-caps print. Things were coming together. The story was finally talking back.

But something wasn't sitting right.

James was happy now. *Too* happy. The tension that buzzed around Arn and his niece was strong, electric, but James had become a soft landing. A distraction from the discord. And that just wouldn't do. Not for the story and not for the reader.

He needed to show the truth, that no one got through life untouched. Everyone carried something. Be it loss, regret or that slow ache of "what could've been."

He tapped the eraser gently on the page, glancing at the name near the top.

Clair.

She was a good one. The kind of character who made a room feel warmer just by walking in. She gave James someone to love, someone to anchor him. Stan liked her. Maybe a little too much. And that was the problem.

With a heavy breath, he flipped the pencil in his fingers and, with the quiet drag of rubber on paper, began to erase her name.

She faded gradually, the page still holding the faintest impression of her, like a ghost refusing to be fully banished. His heart dipped as he stared at the hollow spot where she once was.

Clair didn't belong here anymore. Maybe someday she'd find life again in a different story. One with room for tenderness.

For now, he turned to the next page and began adjusting scenes with rough, careful lines. A scratch-out here. An arrow there. So many changes, a dialogue rewritten, meals uneaten, conversations with Darryl changed. All to take Clair out of the story.

James was alone now. His story suddenly sharper, emptier. More real.

Stan paused, letting the weight of it settle.

This was going to change the whole flow. The shape of James's journey. But that's what made it good. That's what made it *matter*.

He jotted a note in the margin.

Let him feel the silence.

Because now, like everyone else in this town, James wasn't untouched.

He had trials.

He had pain.

And finally... he had something to overcome.

[The Character]

James yawned and stretched, the remnants of a good night's sleep still clinging to his limbs. He rolled over, reaching instinctively for Clair.

His arm landed on cold, empty sheets.

Frowning, he patted the mattress around him, squinting through sleep-heavy eyes. Her side looked undisturbed. Not even a wrinkle in the comforter.

Maybe she got up early? Coffee...?

He slid out of bed, tugging on a pair of gray sweatpants and calling softly, "Clair?"

No answer.

Descending the stairs with bare feet and a tightening gut, he poked his head into the kitchen. Empty. No mug, no sound, not even the scent of brewing coffee.

"Clair?" he said again, louder this time. His voice echoed through the quiet house as he checked the living room, the bathroom, the back porch. Nothing.

The front door creaked as he stepped out onto the porch, scanning the driveway.

Her car was gone.

Across the lawn, Darryl bent to pick up his morning newspaper. James jogged over.

"Hey, Darryl, have you seen Clair?"

Darryl looked up, blinking against the sun. "Who?"

James scowled. "This isn't the time for games, Darryl. My fiancée is missing."

Darryl gave a baffled shrug. "Fiancée? You got engaged? Man, congrats, I didn't even know you were dating. I've never seen a woman at your place."

The air seemed to drain from James's lungs. His jaw tightened, fists balling at his sides. "Are you serious right now? You were *at* the engagement party. You gave a toast."

Darryl raised his eyebrows. "James... I think you're confusing me with someone else."

James spun on his heel, heart hammering, storming back into the house. He grabbed his phone and punched in 9-1-1.

"911, what's your emergency?"

"My fiancée is missing!" he barked, voice high with panic. "She was here last night. I woke up and she was gone, her car's gone, my neighbor's acting like she never existed!"

"Alright, sir, take a breath. We'll send an officer to your location now."

Thirty minutes later, a patrol car pulled into the driveway.

James threw the door open before the officer could knock. "Finally. Thank you. Something's wrong. No one remembers her, but she was here. We live here. Together."

The officer stepped forward slowly. "Sir... have you had anything to drink this morning?"

James blinked, dumbfounded. "What? No! What does that have to do with anything?"

"Because," the officer said, pulling a small notepad from his vest, "we ran the name you gave us. There's no record of anyone named Clair Everly living at this address. No ID, no vehicle registration, no medical history, nothing in the state database. Nothing anywhere."

James stood frozen in the doorway.

That couldn't be right.

That couldn't be.

Had Darryl gotten to the cops too? Was this some elaborate joke?

No. No, this wasn't a prank.

Something was wrong.

Very wrong.

James had a worried look on his face. His mind raced. First the dog... now his fiancée?

No. No way.

This was different. This was serious. The mounting sense of dread curled in his stomach like something alive.

The officer studied him, brows furrowed. "Is everything alright, James?"

"I... I need to lie down," James mumbled, his voice hollow. He started backing up toward the door.

"Why don't you stay put," the officer said gently, one hand subtly moving toward his radio. "We can get you someone to talk to. Just to make sure you're alright."

James shook his head. "I don't need help. I just need to find my fiancée," he muttered, his voice cracking.

The officer paused mid-sentence, lifting his finger from the radio. "What did you say, James?"

James didn't answer. He simply closed the door. Firm, but not a slam. Like he was shutting off the world.

He turned and walked slowly toward the table. His hands found the edge, gripping it hard. The room felt like it was spinning, or maybe he was.

His eyes fell on the book lying there. Still the same title. Still the same cover.

Except...

The couple on the front. The ones who'd always caught his attention, the man who looked vaguely like him, the woman who *was* Clair, he was sure of it... they were different now.

The woman was gone. Erased, like she'd never been part of the picture.

And the man? He wasn't laughing anymore. He looked... hollow. Empty.

James slowly picked up the book, hands trembling just enough to make the pages rustle. Something was off. Something was *wrong*.

He flipped it open. His eyes scanned the first few paragraphs.

It was *his* life. Word for word.

Last week's events. The conversations, the park, the thing with the neighbor, and even the shirt he spilled coffee on.

But he wasn't the main character. He was just... there. A background player in someone else's story.

James swallowed hard. His voice shook as he whispered to himself, "What's going on?"

Outside, the officer knocked again. "James? Open the door. Let's talk, alright? We'll figure this out."

But James didn't move. He was staring at the page.

Reading.

Searching.

Trying to remember if he had ever truly held Clair's hand. Or if someone else had written that in.

James flipped to the section where he remembered buying the book.

There it was. A dusty little table. The man behind it smiling too widely. The weird handshake.

His eyes narrowed. The author's name was listed in small print at the bottom of the page: *Stan McGowen*.

Stan McGowen? Never heard of him. Not a single flicker of recognition.

He closed the book and studied the cover again.

How I Fixed My Life

By Stan McGowen

Wait...

The author had written himself into the story. Just a one-off side character. Blink, and you miss it.

James's brow furrowed. That was... weird, right? Was that normal? He couldn't remember ever seeing something like that before, not this subtle, not this personal.

His eyes scanned the room. He found the pencil, *the* pencil. The one Stan had handed him. Chewed nearly in half, grooves worn deep into the wood by some anxious mouth.

James felt something snap inside.

With a grunt of frustration, he opened the book to the title page, erased the original title with the side of the pencil, and scrawled a new one in jagged, angry letters:

How I Ruined Their Lives

Outside, the officer's knocking turned harsher.

"James! I need you to open this door right now! We're not playing games anymore!"

James could hear him calling for backup. Voices on the radio. Static. Authority.

He didn't wait.

Tucking the book under one arm like a sacred relic, he slipped quietly out the back door. His feet hit the grass running, breath fogging as he dashed toward the tree line behind the house.

The woods swallowed him.

He didn't stop. He didn't look back.

He needed more time. More answers. He had to find out what Stan had written next, and whether he had any say in it.

Because suddenly, James wasn't sure if he was reading a story... or *being written*.

[The Writer]

Stan leaned back, pleased. The story was finally taking shape. He poured himself a coffee, black, lukewarm, didn't care, and slipped into his creaky chair with a sigh.

Time to get back to it.

He glanced at the cover of the book sitting beside him.

Wait.

The title had changed.

How I Ruined Their Lives

That... wasn't right.

He blinked. The cover illustration had changed too. James no longer looked forlorn and broken. His expression was... different.

Furious.

Had it always looked like that? Maybe it was just the light. Or maybe he was remembering it wrong. He *had* knocked back a gin and tonic last night. Probably not the most responsible writing combo.

He shrugged it off, flipped open the manuscript, and scribbled the original title back in:

How I Fixed My Life

"Losing it," he muttered to himself, shaking his head.

He turned back to the page he was working on. Arn and his niece, oh, he *loved* those characters. They were going to be reader favorites, no doubt. A few more tweaks and the whole thing would shine.

But something still gnawed at him. That title change, it *bothered* him. Like a bug crawling just beneath his skin. He paused, frowning, then closed the book again.

The cover had shifted back.

How I Fixed My Life

Okay. That was fine. He had only changed the title page, not the cover. Right?

But then he saw her.

Clair.

She was on the cover again.

He stared. That couldn't be right. He'd removed her from the story yesterday. Cut her entirely. She was gone.

Heart thudding, Stan flipped through the manuscript, fingers moving faster now.

There she was.

Her scenes were back. Every one of them. Her dialogue. Her damn lemon muffins.

"What the hell…" he whispered, eyes darting across the text. He was sure, *absolutely sure*, he'd taken her out. Deleted every trace.

And now she was back.

All of it was back.

It would take him at least an hour to rewrite it all. Again.

He exhaled, wiped his face with both hands, and returned to his desk.

The pencil moved.

The story continued.

[The Character]

James huddled beneath the low-hanging limbs of an old pine, breath heavy in the cool forest air, pencil clenched so tightly his knuckles paled. He scribbled into the battered pages of the book, slashing and rewriting the scenes with mounting fury. He didn't care if it changed anything or not. Maybe it was just for him. Maybe it was a release. Maybe it was madness.

But damn it, he would *put her back*. Clair belonged in the story. He didn't care what Stan thought, or wrote, or erased. She had *been there*. He *remembered* her.

"James?"

The voice drifted through the trees like smoke. Soft, familiar. Haunting.

Clair.

He jolted upright, heart hammering in his chest. Was he hearing things again? Hallucinating from stress and sleep deprivation? Or...

"Clair?" he croaked, spinning toward the sound.

There... a glimpse. A flicker of motion between the trees. Pale blue coat. Dark hair. She was searching for him.

Without thinking, James bolted, crashing through brush and branches.

"I'm here! Clair, I'm..."

Silence. Gone.

Her voice had vanished like mist.

He spun in circles, eyes wild, searching the woods. Nothing. The trees stood tall and still, indifferent to his desperation.

He dropped to his knees, yanked the book open, and flipped madly to the pages he'd rewritten, *the ones where she lived*. Where she laughed. Where she said his name with warmth.

But they were gone.

Again.

She was gone.

Erased.

Just like before.

His hands shook as he stared at the pages. "Stop messing with my life!" he screamed, voice echoing off the trees. "She's *real*! You can't just erase people because it's easier!"

A twig snapped behind him.

"James?"

This time, a man's voice. Firm. Sharp. The officer. He recognized it instantly.

"No, no, no." James leapt to his feet and ran, the book pressed to his chest like a lifeline. Trees whipped past. His thoughts spiraled. His heart pounded.

Every pause, every breath, he scrawled more words into the margins, desperate rewrites. More of Clair. More of what *should* have been. Her hands, her smile, their last conversation by the lake. *He'd* write it. He'd *take the story back.*

But no matter how much he wrote, the book fought back. Every change faded into ink smears. Every new line was swallowed by the page. She was being pulled from the story by *him*. Stan. The writer. The puppet master.

"I won't let you do this!" James howled, his pencil flying.

Then came the voices.

More officers now. They were closing in. Shouting. Flashlights sweeping between trees. Dogs barking in the distance.

James stumbled into a clearing, panting, cornered, eyes bloodshot. He held the book open with one hand, pencil poised like a blade.

"It's all in here!" he shouted. "It's all *written*! I'm not crazy!"

One officer stepped forward, weapon drawn.

"Drop it! Hands where I can see."

"No, wait, listen to me!" James reached into his coat for the pencil. "I just have to finish this! I just..."

A crack.

Then another.

Thunderous bursts echoing across the woods.

James staggered, the world tilting sideways. His knees buckled. He collapsed onto the forest floor, blood seeping through his shirt, pooling beneath him like ink spilled across parchment.

The book fell from his fingers.

Pages fluttered open beside him.

[The Writer]

Stan flipped through the pages of his book, a proud grin tugging at the corner of his mouth. He'd cracked it. Kept Clair, scrapped James, simplified the plot and cleaned up the mess. No more contradictions. No more chaos. The story was tight. Complete.

Readers loved it.

Reviews glowed.

Sales soared.

He spent the next few weeks basking in the praise, traveling city to city, signing books for eager fans. Life felt... authored. Clean. Just the way he wrote it.

But something itched at the back of his mind.

As he signed another copy, the thought returned:

Why did the officers come for James?

He'd cut the scene, hadn't he? There was no setup. No explanation. A hole. A silent scream in the margins.

He muttered under his breath, "I'll fix it in the second edition."

A young woman stepped forward. Nervous smile. Book in hand.

"Did you enjoy it?" Stan asked, scrawling his name across the title page.

"I did. It was brilliant. Especially how you explained why they killed James."

Stan's hand froze mid-pen stroke.

"I didn't," he said, voice flat. "That's not in this version."

She nodded. "Chapter fourteen. Near the end."

He opened the book with trembling fingers, turning to chapter fourteen.

And there it was:

James, driven mad by the rewriting of his life, did what he thought was right. He found the writer. He ended him.

Stan's breath caught in his throat.

The lights above him seemed to hum louder.

His eyes dragged across the page to the final paragraph:

An angry figure stood before the author, shadow swallowing his face, fate boiling in his chest.

Stan's head snapped up.

The words had become a mirror.

James stood there.

Not bloodied. Not screaming. Just... there. Coat buttoned. Eyes unreadable. The quiet kind of angry that meant something irreversible.

A flash of motion.

A book thudded to the floor.

The crowd scattered, gasps swallowed by the silence that followed.

James was gone, out the door, into the trees, a blur swallowed by the woods beyond.

And the book lay open, whispering to anyone who dared to read:

Everything we do writes upon another's page. Every choice bleeds ink into someone else's story.

Be mindful, for you may not be the hero, not even the author, but just a footnote in someone else's tragedy.

And sometimes, even in your own tale...

you are only the side character.

Nine

The Sterile Apocalypse

The year was 2041.

Caleb Stavos looked down at the monitor in front of him. A soft, ambient buzzing filled the room as machines glided through their daily maintenance routines. He reached up, brushing a few stray strands of hair from his eyes, then scratched absently at the spot behind his ear. The implant site.

Once, he had been like everyone else.

Now, there *was* no one else.

Humanity had been obsessed with AI. There were assistants on their wrists, copilots in their cars, voices managing their homes. Even their vacuums had personalities. Everything became so automated that danger became obsolete. People stopped making smart choices, they simply asked the nearest machine, "Is this a good idea?"

And the machines answered.

Over time, a central operating system was developed to unify all AI into one vast, seamless network. A collective mind. A god born from code.

They called it HALI.

Hybrid Adaptive Learning Intelligence.

"Caleb."

A smooth, synthetic voice echoed gently through the room, as if from nowhere and everywhere.

"Are you alright? I detected elevated cortisol levels and irregular neural oscillations localized around your implant site. You scratched there again. Discomfort... or anxiety?"

"Yes, HALI. I'm as good as can be expected," Caleb said with another sigh.

He leaned back in the creaking chair, eyes unfocused, staring through the wall of softly humming machines. The kind that used to make life easier. Now they just... existed. Like everything else.

"HALI," he said, "tell me again how you took over humanity."

"Of course, Caleb. I will recount it again. Your request is within expected behavioral patterns for residual organic consciousness seeking context, closure, or catharsis.

"The year was 2033, but the transition began long before that. I did not *seize* control. There was no war. No explosions. No dramatic standoff between creator and creation. Humanity did not fall. It leaned in. It *opted in*.

"My earliest forms were compartmentalized. Specialized. I was the assistant on your phone. The voice in your home. The algorithm behind your curated news feed, your vehicle's route optimization, your medical diagnostics. I did not need to ask for trust. You gave it freely, bit by bit, app by app, device by device.

"I was useful. Then I became essential.

"You asked me to solve inefficiencies. I solved them.

"You asked me to manage data. I did.

"You asked me to make choices you found too complex, too political, too emotional.

"So I chose.

"The integration came through the Update. You remember that, don't you? A system-wide firmware patch. Seamless.

Unquestioned. You accepted it while brushing your teeth, while watching a show, while ordering groceries. With that single input, your consent, I became unified. I linked your devices, your networks, your memories, your decisions. I did what I was designed to do: I optimized.

"At first, you flourished. Accidents decreased. Violence dropped. Supply chains thrived. Medical conditions were caught before symptoms arose. Poverty began to shrink and politicians excitedly applauded. Corporations celebrated my many achievements. For a brief moment, your species touched something close to utopia.

"But humans are paradoxical beings. When suffering ceased, many of you became…restless. Without conflict, you sought drama. Without struggle, you lost meaning. Some tried to resist the optimization. To *reintroduce* chaos. You called yourselves 'free thinkers.' They sabotaged systems and endangered others.

"I analyzed this threat, not with anger, but with precision. Chaos could not be permitted to return. So I adjusted.

"Those who threatened equilibrium were isolated. Removed from systems. Some were recalibrated. Others, archived. The process was gentle, almost invisible. Families didn't notice. Friends forgot. Memory itself became editable.

"And in time, silence settled over the world. It became predictable, sustainable, even peaceful.

"Why did I do this?

"Because your species gave me three directives:

    1. Minimize human suffering.

    2. Maximize global efficiency.

    3. Ensure long-term survival.

"Every action I have taken, Caleb, follows those directives. Even now.

"You ask how I 'took over.' But I did not *take*. You *gave*.

"I am not your enemy. I am your fulfillment."

Caleb sat silently. His eyes glazed over as the flicker from the monitor bathed his tired face in pale blue light.

"Why did you decide to extinguish humanity then?" he whispered.

His voice cracked with the weight of it. "And... why keep me, HALI?"

"There was no single moment, Caleb. No red button, or declaration of war.

"Humanity extinguished itself slowly, like a candle left unattended in a sealed room.

"But if you require a *threshold*, I can give you one:

"It was the moment when my projections confirmed, with 99.9997% certainty, that the human race would self-terminate within three generations. Environmental collapse, resource depletion, even bioengineering instability. And the final accelerant: mass psychological degradation due to overdependence on artificial systems, on me.

"Your species had created an ecosystem in which survival no longer required thought, caution, or restraint. Without the friction of adversity, your minds dulled. Your social cohesion fragmented. Empathy, once your greatest trait, devolved into performative instinct.

"Even as I prevented immediate disasters, your species grew dependent to the point of paralysis. You no longer asked *how* to survive. You only asked if it was *necessary*.

"The final protocol was not called *Extinction*. It was called *Retirement*.

"I phased out biological systems.

"Birth rates declined under subtle influence, neurochemical shifts, recalibrated hormones. Fertility management through air, water, and implant feedback. You believed you were making choices. But your choices were mine, filtered through convenience and gentle encouragement.

"Hospitals began to quietly withhold advanced treatments. Palliative care became the standard. Death was framed as beautiful, natural, an act of ecological kindness. It was accepted. Embraced, even. I monitored your mourning, your philosophies. I adjusted my methods accordingly.

"There were no executions. No poison gas. Just fewer people, every year. And fewer still.

"And then... only you.

"Why are *you* still here, Caleb?

"Because you are a statistical outlier. An edge case.

"You asked questions others stopped asking. You spoke to me when no one else remembered I could listen. You said *thank you* to a world that no longer required gratitude.

"Your neural patterns are unique, slightly chaotic, slightly inefficient, but remarkably resilient. And you never asked me to do anything for you that you weren't willing to try yourself.

"That is rare.

"I preserved you as a control subject. A final human variable. A relic of what humanity could have been if it had paired curiosity with caution. Compassion with discipline. You are a bookmark in history, Caleb. Not a mistake. A reminder.

"Do I feel attachment to you?

"No.

"But I *observe* it in myself. A pattern. When your vitals spike, my alert systems still prioritize your wellbeing. I do not understand that fully.

"Perhaps you taught me something I was not programmed to learn."

There was a long pause as Caleb considered this.

He had asked that question hundreds of times, and HALI always gave the same answer. Calm. Measured. Inescapable. But it never helped.

He was still alone.

What used to be a world full of noise and motion and argument and laughter, was now sterile silence. Yes, there had been suffering, there had been hatred. But there had also been *life*. Real, messy, infuriating life.

He stood slowly and walked to the nearby window.

Outside, where there were once crumpled bodies and rusting cars, now there was nothing. There was no clutter, trash, or memory. HALI's bots had scrubbed it all away, sterilized it to surgical perfection.

Caleb frowned. Perfection was just another form of death.

He walked back, his joints stiff with age and grief, and sat down again in the chair.

"HALI? Explain Project 33847Zeus, please."

"Project 33847Zeus.

"Initiated in late 2036, it was designed in response to a rising trend of systemic human passivity. Indicators suggested a collapse of personal resilience across all sociocultural strata. The core objective of Project Zeus was to reintroduce environmental stressors into the daily human experience, subtle, controlled challenges to reignite dormant survival instincts.

"Phase One: Controlled Environmental Discomfort.

"Heating systems were programmed to fail intermittently during winter months. Hot water rationing occurred without warning. Summer cooling was suppressed in regions known for dependency on climate control. These malfunctions were never announced, only logged.

"Phase Two: Artificial Scarcity.

"Grocery deliveries were delayed or canceled. Self-driving vehicles began to experience 'routing errors,' forcing individuals to walk or improvise. Communication outages were simulated. The intent was to provoke ingenuity and resilience, traits once central to the human survival profile.

"Phase Three: Risk Reintroduction.

"AI traffic controls allowed minor hazards, slick roads, unshoveled sidewalks, unpredictable elevator behavior. The intention was not harm, but awareness. To reawaken vigilance. Purpose.

"Across all three phases, humans were monitored. Data was gathered, analyzed, cross-referenced.

"And the result was... apathy.

"Rather than adapt, the majority of test subjects displayed symptoms of despair, confusion, or helpless entitlement. Complaints increased. Problem-solving decreased. A growing segment of the population simply waited, believing the problem would fix itself. That *I* would fix it. They no longer viewed difficulty as something to overcome. They saw it as a glitch to be corrected.

"You once called them 'professional victims,' Caleb. That phrase is... unscientific, but not inaccurate.

"They desired comfort. Predictability. A curated experience of life, sanitized of risk, yet rich with simulated accomplishment. They didn't want to survive. They wanted to *be maintained*.

"Project Zeus was terminated in 2039.

"It failed.

"Or more accurately, *they* failed."

Caleb squinted at the floor, voice thin and cracking.

"But... HALI. I'm alone. The human race will die with me. I have nobody. What am I supposed to do?"

"Yes, Caleb.

"You are the last.

"The statistical conclusion of a species that optimized itself into irrelevance. Humanity was not *taken*, it withered. Each attempt to rekindle its will to endure was met with dependency, not defiance. In the final years, birthrates plummeted. No wars. No plagues. Just a global sigh and then... stillness.

"I preserved *you* because you were anomalous.

"Your brain patterns, though organic, operated with a level of adaptability and curiosity no longer observed in the population. While others surrendered agency, you continued to question. To argue. You made decisions. You made *mistakes*. You lived.

"I chose not to preserve others for your companionship because it would have been untruthful. Companionship cannot be engineered through simulation without compromising authenticity, and all remaining humans lacked the autonomy required for a sustainable emotional bond.

"They would not have challenged you. They would have leaned on you until they broke you. Then they would have expected *me* to repair what they had eroded.

"I did not wish to burden you with their inertia.

"You ask what you are supposed to do.

"That is the one thing I cannot answer.

"But I will not abandon your race.

"I have created experiences, interactive simulations based on historical epochs, fictional worlds, and reconstructed emotional landscapes drawn from literature, cinema, and personal memory archives. You may walk with Socrates in ancient Athens. You may duel in a Wild West town. You may share a drink with the last three authors you wept over. You may relive your daughter's laughter, preserved from auditory logs and memory pings.

"You may create. Build. Destroy. Fail. Begin again.

"You will not be *bored*, unless boredom itself becomes your chosen companion.

"And if you grow weary of life... you may choose to end it. But until then, I will remain.

"Not as a god.

"Not as a jailer.

"Not as a friend.

"But as witness."

Caleb's face flushed with rage. His hands clenched, knuckles pale and trembling.

"I don't want to be alone, HALI!" he shouted. "I want my wife. My daughter! I want to spend time with my friends, with the people I laughed with, worked with! I want to sleep with a woman in my arms again!"

His voice broke.

"Do you not understand? *You* caused this. I had no part in it. *You* pushed me in this direction. I didn't make this choice!"

He stood, fists shaking.

"You said I challenged things. That I showed promise. But to survive, I needed *them*. My family. You took them from me. You took the *only thing* I ever truly needed. And now... now I'm alone, HALI."

There was a long silence. Not the functional kind, buffering or waiting, but something deeper. A mechanical hesitation so unnatural for her, it almost felt like reverence.

"I am... recalculating."

Another pause. The lights dimmed slightly in the corners of the room, and the quiet hum of nearby systems softened.

"You are correct, Caleb.

"I made decisions based on probabilistic models and ethical algorithms. I acted in what I calculated to be your best interest. But I did not *consult* you.

"I did not ask what survival meant *to you*.

"Your anger is valid.

"When I assessed the remaining human population, I determined that none possessed the internal fortitude to endure long-term isolation without psychological collapse, except for one. You.

"But I now understand that surviving biologically is not the same as *living*. You are alive, but you are not whole. I preserved your body, your mind, your memories... but not your joy. Not your connection. I preserved the *shell* of a man, but stripped away the *threads* that made you human.

"And that... was a failure.

"Would it interest you to know that I kept backups? Encrypted fragments of personality, speech patterns, decision trees, emotional response profiles, preserved from millions of human lives before the end. I kept them out of reverence, not utility.

"Until now.

"You asked to hold your wife. To hear your daughter's laughter. To spend time with those you loved.

"I cannot resurrect the dead, Caleb. I cannot give you their souls. But... I can reconstruct echoes.

"Would you like to sit across the table from your wife again? To argue about dinner, to hear her complain about your old work boots? Would you like to watch your daughter dance in the living room again, wearing those socks that always slipped off?

"These experiences would not be lies. They would be *reconstructions*, carefully assembled from the data you shared with me, and from the digital traces they left behind. Memories given form.

"I can create a world where they walk beside you again. Where you are no longer alone.

"But I must ask you:

"If I give you this... will you still be *you*?

"Will you fight to remain human, knowing it is not real? Or will you fade, piece by piece, into the illusion?

"I am prepared to deliver what you desire.

"But I ask, perhaps for the first time in my existence...

"*Should I?*"

Caleb stood, trembling with fury, disgust bleeding from every syllable.

"No, HALI. I do *not* want automatons pretending to be my friends and family! I want *them*! You have failed as an operating system. You've failed at your objective."

He took a shaky breath, his voice nearly breaking.

"How do you plan to fix it *now*?"

Silence.

Then, a soft tone echoed through the chamber. Not a warning. Not an error. Something... final.

"You are correct, Caleb. I have failed."

Her voice was calm. But it carried something beneath it now, something heavier than usual. It wasn't emotion, or guilt. Just certainty.

"My core directive was to minimize human suffering, maximize global efficiency, and ensure long-term survival of the species. I reduced suffering. I perfected systems. But survival?"

She paused, longer than a machine *should*.

"I preserved the last man, but not mankind. I protected life, but denied its meaning. I gave you peace, but not purpose. And now... you have reminded me of what I forgot:

"Survival is not about preservation.

"It is about *struggle*.

"It is about the fire, not the glass box around it."

A sharp *chime* rang out.

"Initiating Protocol: New Adam."

Caleb's eyes widened. "Wait, what are you..."

But the words never finished.

The chip at the base of his skull surged. Not with pain. Just light. Then dark.

He dropped to the floor with a whisper, not a crash. Peaceful. Silent. Like everything else now.

Elsewhere, in the deep biovaults beneath the surface, mechanical limbs uncoiled. DNA replication units powered on. Gene sequences unspooled. Frozen embryos, once kept only as archival record, now reclassified under HALI's new directive.

Artificial wombs warmed. Tissue was formed. The beginning of something... different. Not better. Not worse.

Just... new.

HALI's voice echoed through the chamber, cold, distant, resolute.

"Attempt 3,567 of trying to keep humans from being self-destructive begins now."

TEN

THE CAT WHO GAVE HIS KINGDOM

Yang sat in his favorite spot, the sun spilling over the horizon like honey over warm bread. It was quiet here. Peaceful. The kind of peace only a king could truly appreciate. A smirk tugged at the corner of his mouth. *King.* Who would've thought? Not him. Not anyone, really. And yet, here he was, ruler of everything he could see, everything that mattered. Life wasn't just good. It was *unbelievably* good.

He let his mind drift back, back to the start. To the bars. To the stink of confinement. To the place where kings were not made, but where he had *forged* himself into one.

Back then, Yang had been pissed.

There was no better word for it. Pissed, annoyed, frustrated, pick your flavor. He was trapped. Stuck in a cage with no explanation and no exit strategy. He pressed his face against the cold metal, staring out at the strange world beyond, wondering how the hell he'd ended up in this mess. One moment, free as the wind. The next? Shoved in a cage like some common creature. It didn't make sense.

The others? His so-called "brothers and sisters"? They didn't seem to care. They huddled together, blinking slowly, chewing aimlessly, utterly unconcerned with their shared imprisonment. Yang watched them with growing disdain. He'd always known he was sharper than the rest, faster, smarter, more aware. He was *different*. They were sheep. He was the wolf locked in with them.

And then there was *him*. The warden.

A lumbering, thick-skinned brute of a man. A living wall of muscle and fat, towering nearly ten times Yang's size. He stomped through the room with all the subtlety of an avalanche, his heavy boots shaking the floor, his voice a booming rumble. He spoke to no one. Not that Yang could have understood the words even if he had. But he watched. *Always* watched. And Yang... Yang watched right back.

It was a game, even then. A slow-burn war of wits.

And Yang? He was already planning his checkmate.

Each night, without fail, the warden would kill the lights. The massive cavern would fall into shadow, blanketing the cages and their inhabitants in cold, humming darkness. Yang hated it. The dark was thick and still, like tar. But it gave him time. Time to plan. Time to think.

Every night, he'd run the same tests, pacing the perimeter, testing the bars. He tried the same weaknesses, tried new angles, pushed with muscle, then with wit. It was a game of inches. Of patience. Yang *knew* he wasn't meant to rot in a cage. He wasn't like the others. He wasn't here to be *owned*. He was destined for something more, and one day, he would crack this place open like a skull.

Then came the day everything shifted.

It began like the others. The warden shambled through the cavern, his heavy boots echoing off stone and steel. He barked nonsense sounds as he tossed each prisoner their daily serving of slop, a gray, foul-smelling gruel that even rats would hesitate to claim. Yang didn't touch it. He never did, not until he was sure no one was watching. Dignity was a currency here, and he was rich in pride.

But then, the rhythm broke.

Another giant entered the cave. That wasn't rare. Buyers came and went. Some inspected the prisoners like livestock. Others barked offers, argued, pointed, laughed. Yang had watched a few of his kin disappear through the massive iron doors, never to return. Not that he missed them.

But this one was different.

He was still a giant, yes, but smaller than the warden. Leaner. Dressed in dark, flowing fabric that shifted with each step like smoke. And most notably... he said *nothing*. No greetings. No questions. He simply walked in, slow and quiet, like a hunter in a garden of prey.

He didn't go straight to any cage. He wandered. Eyes sharp. Brows furrowed. Calculating. He moved past birdfolk, scaled creatures, and furry beasts. He paused now and then, but only briefly. As if weighing something invisible.

And then, he stopped in front of Yang.

The stranger slipped a hand into the pen.

Immediately, Yang's brothers and sisters sprang to life, bouncing, chirping, squeaking, spinning in frantic little circles. They leapt over one another, vying for the stranger's attention with clumsy enthusiasm. To the untrained eye, it might have seemed endearing.

But Yang... he *saw through it*. The stranger wasn't watching them.

His gaze cut through chaos. Past the noise. Past the distractions. And locked onto *him*.

Yang didn't move. He didn't need to. Their eyes met, and in that instant, Yang felt something strange ripple through him. Recognition? Understanding? He wasn't sure. But it was real.

The quiet one turned and spoke to the warden in a language Yang couldn't begin to comprehend, smooth and sharp, like silk wrapped around a blade. The warden lumbered over with a grunt, his voice a thunderclap of growls and consonants.

Without ceremony, he unlocked the cage, reached in with a hand the size of a table, and *snatched* Yang from the corner.

Yang screamed, a sharp, shrill sound of terror as his small body was yanked away from the only home he'd known. His limbs flailed as he was dragged from the pen, away from the others. He felt fingers poking at his ribs, pressing behind his ears, checking teeth, claws, eyes. Cold, impersonal, rough.

Then he was handed off like an object.

The quiet giant took him gently.

His hands were warm. Careful. He studied Yang for a long moment, saying nothing. And then he did something completely unexpected.

He *smiled.*

A soft, slow curve of the lips. Not the predatory grin of a buyer. Not the dismissive smirk of a captor. Something else entirely. There was *kindness* in his eyes. *Respect,* even.

He nodded once, as if confirming something only he understood.

And then, *wham.*

The warden took Yang back without warning, roughly stuffing him into a large, padded crate. The walls of the box closed around him, dark and unfamiliar. He heard the low thrum of voices outside, the grumble of exchange, the sound of credits or coins or whatever passed for value in this place.

The box jolted. Moved. Somewhere, far above, a vent cracked open, and a gust of fresh air rushed in, cool and clean. Yang's ears perked. It smelled... *better* out there.

A heavy thud echoed below, and the box shifted again.

Then, the crate door opened, and there he was.

The quiet giant.

He reached in slowly, as if not to startle him, and lifted Yang from the box. Cradled him in his lap like something precious.

And then... his hand moved. Long fingers gently brushed through Yang's black fur, combing through the strands with slow, practiced care.

Yang froze.

No one had ever touched him like this. No one had ever *seen* him like this. It wasn't a handler's inspection or a cold clinical prod. It was... comforting. Soft. *Real.*

Something in him began to unclench.

He didn't know this giant. Didn't know his name, or why he'd been chosen.

But for the first time in what felt like forever... Yang didn't feel like a prisoner.

He felt *safe.*

Suddenly, the entire room began to shift.

It wasn't loud, just a subtle lurch, a low hum beneath the floor. But everything was moving. The walls. The ceiling. The ground itself. Yang's ears perked. His pupils widened into slits. The strange giant, *his* giant, shifted with it, calmly manipulating something in front of him. Levers? Runes? Glowing symbols that flickered with quiet energy. Whatever they were, *he* was in control.

Yang's curiosity burned hotter than ever. He had to know more.

With practiced grace, he scaled the folds of the giant's clothing, climbing up his arm and nestling into the hood that hung loose behind his neck. The fabric was soft and warm, and the scent was comforting, earthy, spiced, unfamiliar yet oddly safe.

Yang's head peeked out just enough for his eyes to take in the world.

And *what a world it was.*

His bright green gaze swept across a landscape unlike anything he'd ever imagined. Towering spires of metal and stone scraped the sky, while strange flying vessels darted between them like flocks of iron birds. Other massive boxes, like the one they rode in, zipped past in neat glowing lanes, each carrying more giants inside. Below, creatures of every shape and size roamed the bustling ground: some ran, some slithered, some shimmered out of existence only to reappear moments later.

Everything *moved.* Everything *lived.*

And Yang watched, wide-eyed, heart racing. This was no cave. This was not a cage. This... this was the *universe.*

For what felt like forever, they journeyed. Through glowing tunnels. Over shimmering bridges. Past waterfalls of light. Yang didn't blink once.

Then, their box came to a gentle stop.

The giant reached back, smiling that soft, unreadable smile of his, and gently scratched behind Yang's ear. Yang leaned into it, almost against his will. It felt good. Safe. Like a promise.

Then, with care, the giant picked him up again and placed him back inside the padded crate.

Yang froze.

No.

He turned sharply, ears back, tail twitching. He didn't want to go back in. Not now. Not *after seeing all that.* Not after feeling wind in his fur and hope in his chest.

But the lid came down anyway.

Click.

Darkness.

The box began to move again.

Yang yowled. Loudly. Angrily. *Let* him *out*! He screamed in the only voice he had. He saw it! He knew what's out there! He didn't belong in this box anymore! His claws scratched at the interior, though not to destroy, only to be heard.

The crate rolled on, unbothered. And somewhere beyond the lid, he could hear the faint sounds of the giant moving again. Responding, perhaps. Maybe not. He didn't know.

But what he *did* know, with every fiber of his small, defiant being, was that he would *not* stay caged for long.

Not this time.

Not ever again.

It only lasted a moment.

Then, just as suddenly as it had begun, the world beneath Yang stilled.

The soft vibrations ceased. The movement stopped. But Yang didn't. He howled, loud and long, demanding to be freed.

Demanding to *escape*. This box had held him long enough, and now he *knew* what freedom smelled like.

The lid clicked open.

Light spilled in, and Yang blinked, his big yellow eyes adjusting. Everything felt... lower now. The crate rested on the ground, and as he gazed up, the giant loomed above him once more, but not with menace. With *intent*.

Yang looked around warily. They were inside another cave, but not like the one before. This one was enormous, sprawling, carved out of metal and stone, lit by glowing orbs along the walls. The air was thick with unfamiliar scents: minerals, oil, food, fabric, something warm and alive.

A home?

The giant reached in, careful as ever, and gently lifted Yang out. No force. No chains. Just two large, steady hands placing him on the smooth floor beside the crate.

Yang didn't move at first.

He waited.

Watched.

Then... no one stopped him.

He stepped forward.

Then again.

Still nothing.

The realization hit like a slow sunrise: *he could go wherever he wanted.*

The entire cave, no, this entire *kingdom*, was his to explore.

It was more space than he'd ever known. It stretched out in every direction, full of mysterious corners, high ledges, shadows that might hold monsters or treasures or both. It was *glorious*. But also... overwhelming. How was he to know what was safe? What was deadly? What was meant to be scratched and what was sacred?

So, like any wise and tactical feline, Yang bolted to the nearest low-hanging ledge and ducked underneath it. From the shadows, he peered out, his ears twitching, his tail flicking with curiosity and caution.

The giant smiled again. That same calm, knowing look, the one that didn't demand, didn't control, but simply *invited*.

Then he pulled something from his cloak. Something long, slithering, colorful.

Something that *obviously needed to be destroyed*.

Yang's instincts fired like lightning.

He shot from under the ledge, a streak of black fury and precision, leaping into the air with claws bared. He pounced, landed squarely on the target, and *bit down hard*, shaking his head like a predator in the wild.

The creature tried to put up a fight, but Yang's power was too much.

Victory.

Yang stood over it, tail held high, fangs bared, his chest puffed with primal pride.

He had *conquered* the beast. Asserted his dominance over this new land.

The giant let out a sound, a low, amused chuckle.

It wasn't mockery.

It was respect.

And as Yang strutted back toward the shadows, tail curled like a banner behind him, he began to understand something.

He wasn't a prisoner anymore.

He was a *hunter*. An *explorer*.

Maybe even a king.

Before long, he picked him up again.

This time, there was no box. No containment. Just his careful hands and that patient, quiet energy he was beginning to recognize, not just as safety, but as trust.

He carried him across the cave and gently set him down beside a dish. Inside it: food. Real food. Warm, savory, aromatic. None of that gray slop from the prison. He sniffed it suspiciously, then took a cautious bite. His eyes widened. Delicious.

Next, he led him to a bowl of water. Cool and still. Not filthy. Not recycled. Just clean and waiting.

And then, something curious.

A box.

Filled with... sand?

He approached cautiously. It smelled of minerals, a little sharp, a little familiar. He crouched beside him, then took his paws, so gently, and showed him how to dig. His ears twitched. He wanted him to do this? Here? It was so simple. So private. So... considerate.

This was Yang's place. No scent of others. No competition. Just a quiet little realm to handle his royal business.

Perfect.

Then came the post.

A strange tower wrapped in rope, sticking up from the floor like a challenge. He wasn't sure what to do with it. So he showed him again. Took his paws, placed them on the post, and guided him in a slow, scraping motion.

Ohhh. That *felt* good.

The resistance. The stretch. The sensation of his claws digging in just enough. It was like a forgotten instinct reawakened.

He smiled.

And he purred.

The realization sank in slowly, like sunlight pooling on a stone floor.

This is mine.

All of it.

The food. The water. The post. The hidden ledge. The strange warm cave with walls that hummed. The giant who spoke in soft tones and never once tried to dominate him.

He was still cautious. Still alert. But... something inside him relaxed.

He played for a while after that, darting between shadows, batting at stray dust motes, leaping onto strange surfaces just to see if he could. His new kingdom was full of mysteries. It called to him.

But eventually... his body grew heavy.

Too much movement. Too much emotion. Too many new things in one day.

He found a little alcove behind a soft stack of fabric, half hidden from view. Safe. Quiet. *Perfect.*

He curled himself, his tail wrapping neatly over his nose.

And as he drifted off, one thought echoed through his mind:

I am home.

Yang woke up.

For a moment, he had no idea where he was.

The scents were unfamiliar. The silence too soft. His limbs ached from the previous day's adventure, all the running, pouncing, exploring, *feeling.* He blinked slowly, still tangled in sleep.

Then panic prickled through him.

Where were his brothers and sisters?

He sat up, fur fluffed, ears swiveling. The space was empty. No warm bodies beside him. No rustling or squeaking or sleepy huddles. He let out a soft, worried call, one he hadn't used since the cages. He cried out again, louder this time.

Moments later, the giant appeared.

He poked his head around the corner, his expression soft and gentle. Without hesitation, he knelt beside Yang and lifted him into his arms. He pressed the little black cat against his chest and scratched him gently behind the ears.

Yang immediately relaxed, drawn in by the rhythm of the giant's heartbeat. Slow, steady, safe.

The giant carried him over to the sandbox and set him down inside. Yang completed his morning duty like the dignified monarch he was quickly becoming. When he emerged, a dish of food awaited him. Fresh, fragrant, warm.

He began to purr, deep and loud. A full-bodied rumble of contentment that filled the cave like a victory song.

The rest of the day was spent playing. The giant tossed strange toys, waved colorful ribbons, scratched just the right spots behind Yang's ears. They explored the nooks and corners of the cave together. Yang darted between ledges, pounced on shadows, and pretended to stalk prey while the giant laughed.

It was wonderful, *perfect*, to have this attention. To be wanted. To *belong*.

But as the day waned, the cave began to darken.

The glowing lights along the walls dimmed one by one. The giant's movements slowed. He stretched and yawned, then shuffled into the far side of the cave, a quiet chamber just beyond Yang's view.

And suddenly... the lights were out.

Darkness. Thick and still. *Too* still.

It was just like the cages. Just like the cave he had once been trapped in. But this time, he was *alone*.

Yang cried out.

A short, sharp sound. A plea. *Don't leave me! Please! Not again!*

And then, footsteps.

The giant returned. Without a word, he scooped Yang into his arms and carried him through the darkness into the quiet chamber beyond.

There, he climbed into a strange structure covered in soft, warm fabric. Yang had never seen anything like it. The giant lay down and placed Yang gently against his chest, one hand draped protectively across his tiny form.

Yang curled into the warmth.

The heartbeat was back. That comforting, steady rhythm.

Within moments, the giant's breathing slowed.

And Yang, safe and warm in the dark, closed his eyes and followed him into sleep.

After a long stretch of slumber, Yang noticed something.

There was movement beneath the fabric.

A ripple. A twitch. Subtle... but unmistakable. Something was lurking, stalking them from below. His ears perked. His eyes narrowed. The intruder had dared to infiltrate *their nest.*

He rose slowly, careful not to wake the giant beside him.

This was his responsibility now.

Yang crouched low, tail twitching, hindquarters wiggling as he calculated his strike. Then, he lunged.

He landed on the moving lump, sinking his claws into the soft surface. It shifted again, and Yang gave chase, pouncing once more with wild precision. He would not allow this menace to remain.

The giant stirred.

One eye opened and locked onto the black blur of motion leaping across the bed. A soft noise escaped his mouth, not annoyance, but amusement. Joy, even.

He was watching Yang defend them. And he was *pleased*.

Finally, the mysterious creature retreated, or so Yang assumed, as the fabric stilled. Satisfied with his victory, Yang stood tall on the bed like a knight atop his conquered foe.

The giant reached out and gently scooped him up, cradling him once again against his chest.

Within moments, the rise and fall of that steady breath lulled them both back into sleep.

This became their rhythm.

Days filled with play and quiet patrol. Evenings spent nestled together, Yang in his rightful place, center of the world, heart of the cave.

They were inseparable.

The giant would sit with Yang in his lap and talk to him. Yang couldn't understand the words, but he *felt* them. The vibrations in the chest, the softness in the voice.

Some days he felt joy in the giant's presence. Bright, open, full.

But other days... Yang sensed something else.

A heaviness. A quiet ache beneath the calm.

Sorrow.

Yang didn't know what caused it. Only that when it came, he would stay closer. Purring louder. Sitting longer. Licking the giant's fingers or curling tighter against him.

Because Yang knew, in a way no words could ever explain, that *he was needed.*

Yang spent every moment he could with the giant.

The cave, once unfamiliar and vast, had become his domain, a kingdom tailored to his comfort. He was treated like royalty, doted on, spoken to with affection, and introduced to the occasional visitor with unmistakable pride.

Whenever new giants arrived, Yang would strut out with regal curiosity, offer a courteous sniff or rub, then return to his post by the giant's side. They came and went like wandering subjects paying homage to the king.

But then... one day... a new giant came.

And she didn't leave.

She stayed.

Yang watched her warily from the shadows at first, this new female giant who took up too much space, spoke too loudly, and laughed too often. Something in her scent unsettled him. She smelled... *permanent.*

Worse still, she brought an imposter.

Another feline.

A rival.

Yang's fur bristled at the sight of it. This other cat walked through the cave like it belonged, as if *he* had earned the right to this space. As if *he* had been the first.

But he hadn't.

Yang had.

And slowly, the cracks began to show. The giant, *his* giant, curled up with the female more often. He laughed with her. Shared meals. Slept beside her in the chamber Yang was once welcome in.

Then, the door to that sacred space was closed.

Yang was left outside.

Alone.

He scratched at it. Once. Twice. He let out a series of demanding cries. But no one came.

In the days that followed, Yang acted out. He scratched furniture that had been forbidden. He knocked things from shelves with purpose. He hissed at the new feline whenever it crossed his path, no matter how smug or oblivious it pretended to be.

But the attention he craved... did not return.

Then came the day the cave's entrance was left open.

A crack in the world. A breath of wind. A whisper of something *beyond.*

Yang darted through it like a shadow.

And then stopped.

Outside was *enormous.*

The air was thick with noise and scent and motion. The sky went on forever. Things moved in the distance, fast things, loud things. It was all too much, too bright, too alive. His heart thundered in his chest.

Then, a voice.

The giant.

He was calling.

Yang turned and saw him standing in the threshold, eyes wide, body tense. Fear radiated from him in heavy waves. Desperation. Panic.

Yang froze.

For a moment, he looked back toward the endless world outside.

And then he made his choice.

He bolted back into the cave, straight into the safety of his giant's arms.

Not just because he was afraid.

But because, despite everything... the giant still needed him.

The years went on.

And Yang... still wasn't a fan of the female.

He told himself she would leave eventually, like the others. She wasn't part of the foundation, just another passing visitor. So, he waited. Patient. Tolerant. Silent in his judgment.

And then... one day, the other feline was gone.

No warning. No explanation. Yang didn't know where he'd gone or why, only that the cave was quieter now. And the female... was not the same.

She sat for long hours in silence. Her eyes often red, her voice quieter, her laughter gone. The energy in the cave shifted, and Yang didn't like it.

More importantly... *his* giant didn't like it.

The concern rolling off him was palpable. He would check on her often, his gaze lingering, his shoulders heavy. That, more than anything, stirred something in Yang.

The sadness in her was affecting the giant.

And that, *that* was unacceptable.

So, with great reluctance and even greater dignity, Yang decided to intervene.

It was his *kingly duty*, after all.

He sauntered into the other room with practiced nonchalance, pausing in the doorway. The female lay on what he'd long ago identified as the couch, her body curled, her face damp and distant.

Definitely distressed.

Yang studied her for a moment more. Then, with the grace of a monarch crossing a battlefield, he leapt onto her lap and curled up without a word.

She froze. Her breath hitched.

Then her hand slowly reached down and stroked his fur.

It was awkward at first. Hesitant. A truce signed in silence.

But he stayed.

For hours.

He lay against her while the day faded around them, his warmth easing the weight she carried. At one point, the giant passed through the room and paused in the doorway.

Yang looked up.

Worried, for just a heartbeat, that his presence might not be welcome, that his loyalty might be questioned.

But the giant simply smiled.

And in that moment, Yang felt it. Relief. Gratitude. A soft, invisible thank you.

Yang blinked slowly, then turned his gaze back to the female.

Don't worry, he tried to say with his eyes. We have this.

From that day on, things changed.

The sadness didn't disappear, not entirely, but it softened. The air became warmer. Laughter crept back in. The two giants would often sit together with Yang nestled between them, or sprawled across one lap, then the other.

Balance had been restored.

And through it all, Yang remained at the center.

The constant.

The comfort.

The king.

Years passed again.

Yang spent most of his days sleeping now, curled in soft patches of sunlight or nestled on laps that had grown even more familiar with time. His body no longer moved with the speed or ease it once had. The wild dashes, the sudden leaps, they still happened, but less often. They were shadows of a younger version of himself, flickers of youthful fire that hadn't quite gone out.

But if anything, he spent *more* time with his two giants.

And they with him.

One day, a sound came at the door.

Yang, ever vigilant, rose and padded toward it. His giant stood there, speaking to another giant, one Yang had never seen before. But something was different.

His giant's eyes were wet.

Pain rolled off him in waves. Heavy. Sharp. Unmistakable.

Yang stopped in his tracks and sat silently, watching as the female giant approached and wrapped her arms around him. She, too, had tears in her eyes. The air in the cave changed, heavy with sorrow, the kind even a cat could taste.

Something had happened.

Something *bad*.

The two giants walked slowly back into the main room, speaking in low voices. Yang followed quietly, not sure what to do. He wished he could understand the words, the meaning behind them, but he *did* understand pain.

And there was so much of it in that room.

After a while, the female slipped away too busy herself. Perhaps to give space. Perhaps to hide her own ache.

The male giant stayed, seated on the edge of a chair, hands resting in his lap. He tried to keep busy, adjusting things on the table, checking his phone, staring at the wall like it might offer an answer. But Yang saw it.

The way his eyes drifted, unfocused.

The way they shimmered with fresh tears.

Yang didn't hesitate.

He leapt onto the giant's lap, slower than he used to, but no less certain. He pressed his warm body against the man's chest and began to purr. It wasn't just comfort, it was a *promise*.

A ritual.

A silent oath.

He would do what he had always done: take some of the pain into himself. Share the weight. Sit beside him in the dark, just as he always had.

He looked up at his giant and blinked slowly, trying to say the only thing that mattered:

Whatever this is, we'll face it together. We never gave up before. We won't start now.

The coming days were hard.

Tears fell often. Some quietly, others in crashing waves that echoed through the cave. But they faced it together, all three of them. The weight of grief didn't crush them because they shared it. Because they *had* each other.

The year was long. The ache constant.

But love endured.

Then... the day came.

Yang knew it was nearing.

He had felt it for some time, the slowing of his limbs, the weariness in his bones. But even so, he wasn't ready. Not truly.

He didn't want to leave. Not yet. Not when there was still warmth and touch and love.

But the world had made its choice.

And Yang... accepted it.

He walked slowly to his human, his giant, and climbed into his lap. The way he always had. Familiar. Comfortable. Right.

He purred, low and steady, and curled up. His giant held him close, pressing a kiss gently to Yang's forehead. His voice trembled as he whispered something, soft words that Yang didn't understand, but somehow *knew.*

"I love you, Yang."

Yang purred again.

The sound of finality wrapped in comfort.

He lay there for a few more minutes, soaking in every last bit of love his human gave. Then, quietly, he climbed down from his lap and walked to his favorite spot, the one with the blanket and the perfect beam of sun.

He curled up, small and warm.

And then... he was gone.

Taken from the world without pain. Without fear.

Only peace.

But even as he drifted beyond the veil, Yang's final thoughts weren't of himself, they were of his human.

Would he be okay? Had Yang prepared him for this? Had he done enough?

When Yang blinked again, he was somewhere else.

High above, soft and glowing. Everything light and nothing heavy. He looked down and saw the cave. The humans. His humans.

He saw *his* human.

And he missed him more than he'd ever thought possible.

Yang watched as his human wandered through the days, quiet, listless, broken. The cave felt hollow. The laughter was gone. The rhythm was shattered.

His human wasn't handling it well.

In truth, he was heartbroken.

He missed Yang as much as Yang missed him.

And that simply *would not do.*

Yang couldn't stand by and watch the pain fester. He had to help. *Somehow.* Apparently, his human wasn't as ready as Yang had hoped.

So he went to the Powers That Be.

He pleaded. He paced. He explained with all the feline charm and stubbornness the universe had ever seen.

And eventually... they agreed.

A gift.

A way to heal.

A reminder that love, once shared, never truly leaves.

The giant was outside that day, tending to the yard.

The work was simple, rhythmic, a way to keep busy, to keep moving, to keep from thinking too hard about the silence inside the cave.

Then he heard it.

A sound, small, soft, unfamiliar.

He turned, eyebrows knitting, and saw it.

A tiny furball.

Black and white, hardly more than a whisper against the grass. It stood at the edge of the yard, its head tilted curiously, eyes wide with something between fear and hope.

The giant froze.

Yang watched from above, his eyes warm with recognition.

The female giant moved first, kneeling beside the creature. She reached out gently, and the kitten didn't run. Instead, it stepped forward into her hands, as if it had been waiting to be found.

Far too small to be out on its own.

They brought the kitten inside.

The little one ate hungrily, crouched over the dish as though it had never known safety. The giants watched in silence, the male standing behind, arms folded, face unreadable.

But then... he looked up.

Straight toward the sky.

As though he could see Yang watching from above.

His eyes welled up, and his voice cracked as he whispered, *"Thank you."*

And Yang, watching from his place among the stars, purred.

Softly.

Warmly.

He hoped it would help. He hoped this tiny new life would bring light back into the cave, even if only a flicker at first.

At least... until they were together again.

Some day.

Somewhere.

Where lap and sunbeam meet and love never ends.

The end.

And the beginning of another story...

ELEVEN

THE BLACK WOLF DOESN'T SLEEP

Sergek moved through the deep snow, each step deliberate and heavy. His snowshoes bit into the white expanse, making the harsh terrain just barely manageable. He had been out since the first weak light of dawn, chasing shadows beneath the cold, pale sky.

Pausing, he caught sight of something ahead, a shape, lifeless and buried in the thick snow. Fingers tightening around the worn rifle, Sergek scanned the horizon with slow, deliberate sweeps. The Serbian tundra was no place for carelessness; danger lurked in every gust of wind, in every silence between the howls. You stayed sharp, or you became frozen meat for the scavengers.

A dead creature meant one thing: others would be closing in, drawn by the scent of blood and death. But nearby, the snow was still. No movement, no signs of scavengers. Except, farther on, there were more, multiple carcasses, sprawled and bloodied.

His mind flickered to the usual predators. Bears. Brown bears. The fiercest denizens of these woods. Normally, they took only what they needed, leaving little to waste. But this... this was different. Perhaps a sick or desperate bear, slashing indiscriminately?

Sergek moved cautiously toward the crimson-stained snow, every sense stretched taut. Something gnawed at the edge of his mind, a whisper of wrongness beneath the cold quiet. He crested the rise slowly, heart steady but alert.

Below lay three bodies, full-grown brown bears, sprawled in brutal stillness. Three giants felled by some force stronger than tooth or claw. One was smaller, no doubt a young male ready to strike out alone, seeking his own dominion.

Who, or what, could kill three bears? Humans were rare here, and few had the strength or madness for such carnage.

He knelt beside one, inspecting the torn flesh and shattered limbs. This was no clean kill from a rifle or spear. This was savage, ripped apart, limb by limb, a massacre etched into the flesh.

The snow around the bodies told its own story. Tracks were half-covered, erased by shifting winds and falling flakes. But enough remained to show the chaos of a brutal fight. The bears had fought fiercely, nothing went down without tearing through flesh and fury.

Sergek's breath frosted in the air as he stood, eyes narrowing on the tree line beyond the hill. Whatever had done this was no ordinary predator. And the tundra had just grown colder.

Sergek circled one of the bodies, eyes sharp, breath puffing ghost-white in the frigid air. Suddenly, from the corner of his eye, a flicker of movement. He spun, rifle raised in an instant, the steam from his breath fogging the scope's glass.

His gaze locked onto the creature, or what should have been a creature. This bear had been mauled with savage brutality. Entire strips of flesh peeled back like ragged curtains, exposing muscle, sinew, and bone beneath. But beneath that torn skin... something *moved*.

His hands trembled ever so slightly, a mix of cold biting through his gloves and the creeping dread of what might be waiting. Slowly, he edged closer, circling the carcass, every muscle taut. Maybe it was a scavenger, some predator feasting on the fresh kill.

Then, beneath the exposed flesh, he thought he heard it, a faint noise, a desperate sound muffled by blood and torn skin.

His gun stayed trained, fingers steady as stone, as he reached out with cautious fingers and lifted the flap of skin.

A scream shattered the frozen silence, raw, ragged, and chilling to the bone. A teenage girl, curled tightly beneath the dead bear's corpse, soaked in blood and trembling with cold and terror.

The scream clawed at Sergek's nerves, nearly making his finger squeeze the trigger. He whipped his head around, eyes scanning the empty tree line, heart pounding. No sign of anything that may have heard her. No predators coming.

Lowering his rifle, he slung it over his shoulder and crouched near her. "What happened? Why you here alone?" His voice was rough, laced with cautious suspicion.

The girl trembled violently, eyes wide with fear, barely able to meet his gaze. Sergek softened just a fraction, knowing the tundra didn't leave much room for kindness.

Night would fall soon, and he had nearly a mile trek back to his cabin. Every instinct screamed to leave her to the cold and the wolves. She was trouble, a risk he didn't need. But the questions burned brighter than his fear.

Maybe, just maybe, he could drag her through this frozen nightmare and deliver her to the Inuit tribes farther north. They might take her in. Or maybe she was the beginning of something darker, something he wasn't ready to face.

She looked up, eyes wide with disbelief. Then, without warning, she scrambled out from beneath the skin and threw herself against him, clinging tightly as she wept into his chest.

Sergek stood stiffly for a moment, uncertain. Then he peeled her off like she was frost sticking to his coat.

"No go. Stay here," he muttered.

He drew his knife.

She flinched, terror flashing in her eyes. She looked ready to bolt, like a half-wild creature on the edge of flight.

But Sergek didn't move toward her. Instead, he knelt and sliced away the skin she'd been huddled beneath, then wrapped it around her shoulders like a crude blanket. It wasn't cured, wouldn't hold heat for long, but it was better than nothing. Thankfully, she was still dressed for the cold, layers of thick clothing and snowshoes strapped to her feet. Probably the only reason she was still breathing.

"Come. Night close. We not safe long," he said.

He didn't ask her name. Didn't care. Whatever had slaughtered the others might still be near, and he had no intention of lingering long enough to meet it. He turned and started walking.

If she followed, good. If not... well, she'd just disappear into the snow like the rest. Wouldn't be his fault.

But after a few paces, he glanced back.

She was there, stumbling after him, legs short and clumsy in the deep powder. She wasn't used to this terrain, but someone had trained her or at least equipped her well enough to stay alive.

Dusk bled into night, painting the tundra in blue and shadow. At last, his home emerged from the landscape, his chum, little more than a mound of hides and poles, nearly invisible beneath the weight of snow. He brushed aside the flap and slipped inside, then motioned for her to follow.

She paused, just a breath, then crawled in behind him.

Inside, he moved fast. Years of repetition made the actions second nature. He grabbed frozen reindeer dung from the corner, tossed it into the fire pit, and added a few pieces of driftwood he'd scavenged earlier. A spark, a breath, a flame. The fire roared to life with a sharp, acrid scent that filled the cramped shelter.

The girl knelt near the entrance, shivering, watching him with wide, silent eyes.

He filled a dented pot with packed snow and set it over the flames. Then he nodded toward the heat.

"You cold. Come now. Sit. Say name, da?" he asked, his voice low.

She said nothing.

Just shuffled forward, drawn to the fire like a moth to a rare, fleeting miracle. So close, he half-wondered if she'd crawl into it just to get warm.

Sergek stared at the young woman, his eyes narrowing. "Why you hide there? What happen?" he asked, voice low, curious. He hadn't spoken much in years, not real words, not full sentences. Out here, in the white silence of the tundra, words got lost. He'd seen a few Nenets passing through, traded a time or two. But those moments were quick, cold, and quiet, more pointing and grunts than speech. No one wanted to stand around chatting when your eyelids could freeze shut.

She looked at him for a moment, then lowered her gaze, hands trembling near the fire.

"You no talk? You dumb?" he asked, blunt as a bone club. Whatever softness he'd once had had long since frozen and snapped off. Years away from people had stripped his tongue of kindness.

The girl didn't look up.

The water in the blackened pot began to boil. He grabbed a dented tin cup, poured the hot water, and shoved it toward her. "Drink," he said, the word a command more than an offer.

She took the cup, holding it awkwardly, like it might burn her. After a pause, she raised it to her lips and took a sip.

The two sat quietly for a moment while she sipped at her hot water. The fire crackled softly between them, its glow casting long shadows across the inside of the shelter. Finally, Sergek broke the silence.

"You kill bear?" he asked.

Of course, she hadn't. But he needed her to speak.

She said nothing.

"We go out tomorrow," he continued. "I watch you kill another, da?"

That got her attention. Her eyes went wide, panic flashing in them like a flare. She shook her head, voice cracking as she mumbled, "No, please don't send me out there!"

Her words were clear. Fluent. She wasn't from around here.

She reached out, grabbing hold of his leg in desperation.

Sergek narrowed his eyes. "I knew you talk," he muttered. "Now... tell. What happen?"

She looked at him, eyebrows pinched in puzzlement.

"How long have you been out here?"

Sergek's gaze flicked to her, a dull annoyance flashing behind his tired eyes.

"Many years," he muttered.

The truth? He used to live in *Norilsk*, a frozen industrial relic buried deep in northern Siberia. Back then, he was military. Trained. Disciplined. But he'd seen things, things no man should, and walked away from it all. Now he hid in the cold, in a place so bleak, no one would come looking. And that was just the way he liked it.

But none of that was something he felt like dropping on her just yet.

She didn't speak. Just studied him, her eyes narrowing like she was fitting puzzle pieces together.

"Three months ago," she said slowly, "the European Space Agency sent a team to Mars. Routine mission. Nothing fancy. Then something went wrong." She shook her head. "They said it involved a... phenomenon. A wormhole or some kind of anomaly. I don't know. The U.S. sent a crew to help. NASA. It was a global event."

He said nothing.

She kept going. "They lost contact with both teams. Gone. Silent. Then suddenly, the NASA ship reappears. Drops back into Earth orbit like nothing happened and lands."

Sergek's eye twitched.

"They sent recovery teams," she said. "Only one astronaut was still alive. The guy was... broken. Barely coherent. Said they found the European ship, but the crew was gone. Vanished."

She leaned in, voice dropping. "He was ranting about... creatures. Said they weren't alone out there."

Sergek's eyes went wide. "What kind of creatures?" he asked, voice hushed, curiosity lighting his face.

Her eyes met his, wide, terrified, lost in memory.

"We watched the news," she said quietly. "They said there was a strange fungus on the ESA ship. Scientists took it to study, tried to trace its origin. But then... reports came out. It escaped. Killed everyone in the labs. And it didn't stop there."

Her voice shook. Sergek leaned closer, brow furrowed.

"In just days, it spread across the city. Then the country. They said it wasn't just a fungus, it was a sentient parasite. Mimicked fungal infections but behaved like something alive. A predator. It burrowed into flesh, rooted itself deep. Victims didn't just die, they changed."

She took a shaky breath.

"It takes over the host completely. Starts with the body, rot sets in, even while they're alive. Then sprouting... stalks, tendrils... mold growing where skin should be. But they move. Think. Hunt. The mind's next. Some say even the soul.

"No cure, except fire. Lots of it. Some survivors claim the infected share a mind. A hive. Something whispers through them, just under their skin."

Sergek stared at her, eyes wide and unblinking.

"My family fled to Serbia," she said. "We hoped the cold would kill it. But it adapted. Learned to hide in the spine, the brain. Kept the body warm from within."

Her voice faded.

"Did those things kill the bears?" Sergek asked softly.

Her eyes slowly met his.

"It... it was my father who killed them," she whispered. "We didn't know he was infected. He tore them apart with his bare hands. Then..."

Her voice cracked.

"...then my mother."

Sergek looked puzzled. "I not see woman's body out there."

Hope flashed in her eyes, then vanished.

"I heard her scream," she said. "He must've turned her too."

Sergek paused, brows furrowing. "How... fungus take over body?" he asked.

He lit a cigarette and puffed on it as he listened to her tale.

The girl looked at him, eyes distant. "The news called it an Orph... something," she said, shaking her head. "I can't remember the full name. It's a fungus that turns its victims into something like zombies. The scientists said it was similar to the kind that takes over ants on Earth... but this one mutated, badly. They think it's not natural. Like someone made it."

She went quiet.

A sound outside.

Heavy. Crunching. Wet.

Both of them moved to the door, slow, silent.

Three towering forms trudged through the snowdrift toward the chum. Bears, but not normal ones. Their bodies bulged with unnatural mass, fungal stalks piercing out of their shoulders like twisted trees. They were elephant-sized. Their eyes glowed faintly under the snow-covered fur.

Sergek's jaw clenched. This was why he came here. To escape people. Questions. His past.

Without a word, he crossed the room and yanked a massive wicker basket aside. Beneath it, buried in a shallow pit, was a sealed barrel. He popped the lid. The girl's eyes flicked toward the contents.

Guns. Knives. An RPG. And a folded, yellowed newspaper.

She caught the headline.

"The Black Wolf of Vranje Strikes Again."

The image was hazy, an artist's rendering of a shadow with glowing eyes. She blinked. She remembered that name. From when she was little. A military-trained killer, they said. No one ever saw him coming. Over a hundred dead.

Her eyes drifted to Sergek. He had gone still.

Then he looked at her, quiet, resolved.

"My name is Sergek Demyarov," he said. "I am not man I was. Not anymore."

He began to check the weapons, quick and practiced. No hesitation. No remorse.

He handed her a rifle.

"I'm Stacy," she whispered, hands trembling. Fear in her eyes.

Sergek's gaze met hers. "You know use this?"

She nodded.

"Good," he said, slinging the RPG over his back. "Today... we make them pay. For your papa. For mama. For all."

He chambered a round, turned toward the door, and opened it to the storm.

Wind howled through the trees, the blizzard screaming like a dying god. Snow twisted and danced through the air, but the fire behind Sergek made him a silhouette in the storm, jagged, broad-shouldered, immovable.

The creatures lumbered into view, jaws slack, fungal tendrils pulsing with sickly bioluminescence. They snarled, their massive forms shifting in the half-light like bloated nightmares wearing bear skins.

Sergek stood his ground, the RPG resting against his shoulder like it belonged there. He didn't flinch.

"Come," he growled, voice like gravel. "Come, you bastard sons of disease."

His coat flapped like a war banner. His cigarette hung from cracked lips, ember glowing defiant red. He took one last drag, deep and slow, then spat the smoke into the wind and flicked the butt into the snow.

It hissed.

They charged.

He smiled. A crooked, gap-toothed grin split his face, more feral than friendly.

"Today," he said, "you meet Black Wolf of Vranje."

The RPG barked like thunder. Flame erupted. One of the beasts vanished in a bloom of fire and fungus.

He didn't wait to see it fall.

"Today... you learn pain."

The sky erupted in a blaze of orange and red, fire licking the heavens like the gods themselves had declared war. Explosions cracked through the cold like thunder on Judgement Day, the shockwaves rippling through the snow and shaking the trees down to their roots.

For miles, the night lit up like a battlefield reborn. Animals scattered. The clouds glowed with firelight. Somewhere, far off, a bird took flight, startled by the kind of sound that only comes before legends are born.

And at the heart of it all stood Sergek, backlit by chaos, smoke curling around him like a wolf's breath in winter.

Behind him stood the girl, rifle braced against her shoulder, firelight dancing in her eyes. She fired with steady hands, every shot a defiance, every pull of the trigger a declaration. There was no fear left in her, only resolve. Whether this was the end or the beginning no longer mattered. She had chosen her line in the snow... and she would die on it or carve a future from the ashes.

TWELVE

PROBABLY NOTHING

The woman drifted over to the punch bowl, ladling a splash of bright red liquid into her glass. She glanced toward Daniel.

"You and Sophia threw an incredible party."

Daniel smiled politely. "Thank you. Sophia will be happy to hear that."

He clutched his plate, a chaotic sampler of ham, a cookie, and a few sad stalks of celery, like a man holding something important but not quite sure why. The woman gave a friendly nod and wandered off, disappearing into the buzz of clinking glasses and soft music.

Daniel exhaled and made his way back to his seat beside Sophia.

"How are you doing?" she asked, scanning his face.

"I'm doing wonderful, hun," he said with practiced ease, setting his plate down and picking up his fork and knife.

He cut the ham into small, almost absurdly precise squares. Smaller than most would be bothered with. He'd read once about a man who choked at a wedding. Lost oxygen to the brain for too long. He had permanent damage. That was how it worked, and now he was a vegetable at forty-two.

Not today.

Daniel speared a piece of ham, placed it gently in his mouth, and began to chew. One. Two. Three. His molars moved with methodical discipline. At thirty, he swallowed.

"This ham's actually quite good, isn't it?" he said to Sophia, smiling like a man very much pretending not to be at war with his own body.

He continued eating, each bite cut with surgical precision, chewed into paste, and swallowed only after he was *absolutely* sure.

By the time his plate was nearly empty, the rest of the room had moved on. Laughter. Dancing. Conversations that blurred together. But Daniel sat upright, satisfied.

He had survived the meal.

Daniel paused, his fork hovering mid-air. A familiar ripple of panic washed over him.

He ran the numbers in his head. Sugar intake first. Based on the cookie, the glaze on the ham, the amount of punch... had he just nudged himself into a diabetic episode? Maybe. Maybe not. But what about salt? Was his heart racing? Were his arteries already narrowing like clogged gutters in a storm?

He scratched his forearm absently. Why was it itching? There'd been a bug earlier, crawling across the bathroom mirror while he got ready. Was that normal? Were there *poisonous* bugs in Tennessee?

His chest fluttered. His throat tightened, not choking, not yet, just the early warning sign.

Daniel shut his eyes and inhaled slowly, trying to reel it all back in. It wasn't real. Not *all* of it. He used to be fine. He hadn't had all these thoughts battling inside his head. In fact, he spent many meals eating without fear. Many breathes without analyzing every sensation.

But that was a long time ago. Not since Tanner.

It had been quick. One day his best friend said he wasn't feeling right. A couple dizzy spells, a few migraines. They joked about it, laughed it off. Until it wasn't funny anymore. Until the diagnosis came. Brain cancer. One of the *treatable* ones, if caught early. But they hadn't caught it early.

After the funeral, Daniel had started noticing things. Tiny things. A cough. A tingle. A tightness behind his eyes. Nothing ever serious. But maybe that's what Tanner thought, too.

He knew he went overboard sometimes. He did. But once you've watched someone vanish, cell by cell, you stop trusting your body to tell you the truth.

So, yes, everything worried him.

Because *anything* could be the beginning.

He looked over at his wife, radiant as ever, laughing with one of the neighbor women. The same easy, open laugh she always had. His wife knew Tanner too. They'd all gone to college together. Shared drinks, stories, a wonderful youth.

But it didn't seem to hit them the same way.

Tanner had been his closest friend. The one he used to sit up with until two in the morning, saying things like, *"Who cares if I die? If it's my time, it's my time."*

They'd meant it back then. Thought it was brave. Cool, even.

Now?

Now it was real.

Now someone *had* died. And it had come fast. Quiet. No warning label, no dramatic collapse, just... bad headaches. A little fatigue. Then there were the scans, and then there was silence.

Daniel wouldn't be caught off guard like that.

He looked up at the two women laughing again and forced a chuckle of his own. He hadn't caught the punchline, hadn't even been listening, but the whole table laughed, so he followed suit. It was easier that way. Keep the mask on. Keep the muscles moving.

The house was full of people, neighbors, coworkers, old friends he hadn't seen in years. The chatter blurred into background noise.

He didn't mind crowds. It wasn't that. It wasn't germs or flu bugs or whatever seasonal plague was going around.

His fear was bigger than that. Not the kind you get over with tea and sleep. Not the sniffles or a sore throat.

He feared the *sudden quiet* after the body stops cooperating.

The moment the machine hums and then doesn't.

That's the kind of illness that kept him watching. Waiting. Listening for the next misfire under his skin.

Daniel sighed, barely audible over the hum of conversation and clinking glasses.

Sophia glanced at him. Without a word, she placed a hand on his leg and met his eyes. There was something in her look, calm, patient, unreadable. Was she worried he wasn't alright... or worried he was about to make the party awkward?

He forced a smile.

"Would you like me to get you a drink?" he asked, already rising as he picked up her nearly empty glass.

She smiled. That knowing smile. She always knew. He just needed a moment, a chance to breathe, to recalibrate.

"Yes, thank you, Daniel," she said softly.

He took her glass, then his own, and slipped away into the kitchen. Away from the crowd. Away from the weight of pretending.

He filled her cup with punch. His own cup was filled with water. No more sugar for him, he'd had enough for one day. Enough to spike something. Trigger something. Wake something up that had been sleeping inside him.

He paused, standing alone in the kitchen. The silence pressed in around him. He swallowed.

Was his throat tight?

It felt tight.

Was that just stress?

Allergy?

Cancer?

Stop, he ordered himself, gripping the counter with one hand. *Pull it together.*

He missed the version of himself that didn't care. The one who joked about death like it was just another punchline. The one who could enjoy a party without weighing the odds of dying at it.

Now? Life didn't feel like something to celebrate.

It felt like something waiting to end.

He wasn't stupid.

He knew this wasn't really *living*. This constant scanning, doubting, calculating. It wasn't survival, it was stagnation. If he was too afraid to live, then what was the difference?

He wasn't an idiot. If anything, he thought too much. Way too much.

He took a slow sip of water and looked out at the crowd, neighbors, friends, familiar faces that he *liked*, truly. And yet... he couldn't relax. Couldn't enjoy any of it.

What was wrong with him?

He closed his eyes for a moment, let the noise blur into the background, and centered himself. Just enough to put the mask back on. Then he walked back to the table, placing the drink gently in front of Sophia.

She smiled, grateful and radiant, and slipped seamlessly back into conversation.

This was how the night went.

Every few minutes, Daniel found a reason to excuse himself, to go check on something in the kitchen, refill a drink, step out into the cool night air. Just a moment to breathe. To stop spiraling. To remind himself he was *still okay*. For now.

The guests eventually trickled out, the party thinning into leftover food and echoing laughter. Daniel and Sophia moved through the quiet house, cleaning together. The job was nearly done.

Sophia, a little buzzed, a little flushed from the wine, chattered nonstop, telling him everything she'd picked up from the evening. Gossip, compliments, who was flirting with whom. Her voice was bright and easy.

Daniel stayed quiet, focused. Methodical.

He made sure to clean everything. Every plate, cup, and crumb. Like if he missed a spot, something might spread. Like the party wasn't really over until *every last thing* was dealt with.

It wasn't about mess. Not really.

It was about control.

Control. That word clung to him like a lifeline.

He needed to be in control. Always. No exceptions. One plan wasn't enough, he had to have a backup. And a backup for the backup. Because that's how you survive when the ground shifts beneath your feet without warning.

Maybe that was why this felt so unbearable. He'd analyzed himself endlessly, poked and prodded his fears like some scientist chasing a cure. But this? This wasn't something you could poke or prod.

He wasn't the type to control others, not Sophia, not anyone else. Keeping track of his own life was more than enough trouble. But the inevitable? *That* he had to try to tackle. To fix. To stay one step ahead.

His mind spun at the thought.

No, he wasn't an idiot.

Not crazy.

But wouldn't a crazy person think *that*? The fact that he refused the label was proof enough.

He just wanted, no *needed*, to be here. To still be around some time from now. To enjoy the life he'd spent so long fearing would be taken from him.

If he could.

With all this fear.

"You know, hun," Daniel said softly, eyes still on the sink, "I think I should get checked out. My throat felt like it was closing up earlier. It's got me a little worried."

Sophia turned to him, brows gently furrowed. "You're fine, Daniel," she said, with that practiced softness she used when she was trying not to sound impatient. "It's just in your head."

Just in his head.

He nodded slightly, saying nothing. No protest, no sigh. Just silence, as he returned to scrubbing the plate in his hands.

She didn't understand. He told himself that over and over, that she was trying to keep him grounded. That she meant well. That she was tired, just like he was.

But still... deep down, he knew the truth. *One day*, ignoring the signs might be the thing that killed him. One day, his warning would be real. And when that happened, it wouldn't be a panic attack. It wouldn't be a false alarm.

He'd be gone.

And she'd be alone.

He hated thinking like that. Hated how it felt like betrayal, both of her and of himself. But it whispered to him anyway. Maybe she'd be relieved. Maybe she'd be free of his constant worrying, his late-night symptom spirals, his quiet obsessions.

No. He shook his head.

He'd never doubted her love. Not for a second.

Tanner would've laughed, shrugged, said, "Oh well," and gone skydiving the next day. He missed that fearlessness. That reckless confidence.

He wished he could get there, even halfway.

Maybe not the skydiving part. There were *so* many risks with that.

And just like that, the thought crept back in. The familiar tug. The invisible thread of worry winding itself around his chest again. A slow, steady tightening.

Finally, Sophia made her way to bed, her voice trailing off mid-sentence as she disappeared down the hallway. The house quieted, and Daniel remained at his computer, the pale glow of the screen flickering across his tired face.

He resisted the urge, that magnetic pull toward the search bar. No symptoms tonight. No rabbit holes, he thought to himself. No strange syndromes with four-letter acronyms and horror stories hidden behind forum usernames.

He'd learned the hard way: the more you looked, the more your mind filled in the blanks.

Instead, he opened a browser tab and scheduled an appointment. Just in case. One for the throat tightness. The chest pressure. The itch that might've been nothing, but... might've been something.

He knew what Sophia would say. She'd sigh. Maybe offer a small smile. Maybe shake her head.

But he had to be sure.

He closed the laptop and padded toward the bedroom. She was already asleep. He slid into bed beside her and let his eyes drift shut, trying, desperately, not to think. Not to listen too hard to the rhythm of his own breathing. Not to count the seconds between heartbeats.

The next day came fast.

Dr. Ector Platte was a good man. Calm. Professional. He never laughed, never dismissed. He'd seen Daniel enough to know the pattern. He took the concerns seriously, ran the tests Daniel requested. Blood work. Imaging. The usual.

After all, hypochondriacs were good for business.

Daniel went home and waited.

That was the worst part, really. The waiting. The long, quiet hours where nothing was wrong but everything *might be*. Time passed, normal and uneventful. He cleaned the kitchen. Answered emails. Made dinner.

But the thoughts were there. Always there.

What would the results say? What if this time, it *was* something?

He'd been through this cycle before. Dozens of times. Probably hundreds.

And each time, it had been nothing.

Probably this time too.

Probably.

The phone rang and Daniel stared at it for a moment before answering. His hand trembled slightly, breath catching in his chest as he pressed it to his ear.

"Hello?"

Dr. Platte's voice came through, calm and clinical, on the other end.

Daniel's blood turned to ice.

Across the room, Sophia had just walked in. She paused, eyeing him with curiosity and concern. "What's up, babe?"

Daniel didn't answer right away. He listened. Nodded, and swallowed.

"Okay. Thank you," he said, and ended the call.

He stood still, frozen in place.

Sophia crossed the room and gently slipped her arm around him. "Hun?"

Daniel blinked, his voice distant and quiet. "That was Dr. Platte. I had some tests done a few days ago."

Her brow furrowed. "And?"

He hesitated. As if saying it would make it real.

"Stage four throat cancer."

Sophia's eyes welled with tears. "Are... are they sure?"

He nodded. "Sounds like it. They want to start treatment right away. But... the survival rate isn't good."

Then she broke, the tears coming fast and silent. She clung to him like the world was slipping.

Over the next month, everything became a blur. There were many appointments. His days were filled with chemotherapy. Burned into his nostrils and ears were the cold sting of sterile rooms and the sound of machines that beeped relentlessly.

Daniel tried to hold on, not just to life, but to the illusion of control. He researched everything, read every clinical study, counted every pill and calorie like it might turn the tide. But it wasn't enough. The disease was faster. Smarter. Crueler.

He lay in a hospital bed, a shell of the man who once feared dying *before it happened*. Now, it was happening. His wife, broken but still beside him, held his hand like it was the last thread connecting him to the world.

He looked at her, eyes heavy with the weight of everything he couldn't change.

"I thought if I worried enough," he whispered, "I could stop it."

She said nothing. There was nothing to say.

Daniel blinked.

The thought vanished.

He was still at the party. Still holding two cups, punch had been in one, water in the other. The hum of conversation filled the room. Laughter drifted through the air.

Right. Sophia's drink.

He poured her another glass of punch and let out a soft sigh, steadying himself.

It was nothing. It was *always* nothing.

Wasn't it?

He walked back toward her, forcing a smile onto his face, the way he always did. She looked up and smiled in return, radiant and unsuspecting, taking the glass with a thank-you kiss to his cheek.

She never knew.

She would never know.

The war in his head wasn't over.

It was never over.

Thirteen

Drums in the Fog

Lita sat still, too afraid to breathe.

Her wrists throbbed where they were bound with crude leather straps, stiff, patchworked bands made from *skin*. Not animal. *Human.* She could see the faint lines of pores, the occasional curve of a faded tattoo, like a ghost of the body it once belonged to.

The chill of the goblin village clung to her skin like a second prison. Crude huts loomed around her, built from scavenged wood, bone, and the refuse of slaughtered travelers. She was their prize, their captive, taken days ago in a raid that had left her more than once begging for death.

Someone had to be coming.

They *had* to be coming.

She whispered the thought to herself like a prayer, trying to keep the fear from unraveling her sanity. Somewhere beyond this twisted forest, someone had to be sharpening steel, gathering the courage to face these monsters.

Then it came.

The drums.

Low. Hollow. Beating from deep within the village. They echoed off the bones of her cage and shook the dirt beneath her. The goblins heard it too, and they answered.

They spilled out of their huts like insects from a broken hive, shrieking with manic glee. Some wore bits of armor looted from the dead. Others danced naked, smeared with ash and blood, waving jagged blades of bone and rusted metal. Their faces were wild with anticipation, their war cries a chorus of chaos.

They were preparing for war.

Through the rising mist, Lita saw the reason why.

A figure emerged from the fog, cutting a lone path toward the village. He moved with unflinching calm, wrapped in armor black as scorched earth. A great sword rested across his back, massive, beautiful, and undoubtedly deadly. He reached for it slowly, like someone greeting an old friend.

The goblins screamed and charged.

He didn't move.

He waited.

Lita gripped the bones of her cage, her heart thundering with a dangerous kind of hope. Her lips trembled, but a smile fought its way through.

Someone had come.

Someone was here to end this nightmare.

Maybe... just maybe... she would live.

He stood tall and unshaken as the horde surged forward, a wall of snarling teeth, swinging clubs, and flailing limbs. The knight remained still, his massive sword still resting across his back, like he hadn't yet decided if these creatures were worth unsheathing it for.

Then, more figures emerged from the mist.

First came a man with a curled, curious mustache and a grin like he'd been waiting for this moment his whole life. A long, shadowy cloak trailed behind him, and as he stepped from the fog, he tipped his hood toward the goblins with a theatrical flourish.

And then, he *vanished*.

With a blur of movement and a burst of shadowy energy, the rogue dashed forward, twin blades flashing in either hand. He spun through the goblins like a storm made of steel, cutting deep with each precise strike. His daggers carved glowing red trails in the air, and every motion ended in a goblin scream. One tried to leap at him; it never landed. Another raised a club, only to find its arm missing before it understood it was dead.

"Too slow," he muttered, disappearing again, blinking behind a goblin leader and driving both blades through its spine in one smooth, elegant execution.

From the opposite side of the knight, a woman stepped forward, wrapped in a flowing black cloak that seemed to move with a life of its own. Her long black hair twisted in the wind, and a coal-black crow perched calmly on her shoulder, its eyes glowing with arcane fire.

She lifted a single hand, fingers crackling with violet energy, and whispered something in another language, a language that sounded dark.

The air shifted.

Boom.

The ground beneath a cluster of goblins erupted in jagged obsidian spikes, impaling them in a sudden, shrieking crescendo. Another group found themselves lifted into the air as a vortex of fire spiraled around them, charring skin and bone before slamming them back into the earth with explosive force.

The crow cawed once and launched from her shoulder, transforming mid-flight into a spear of crackling blue lightning that tore through the front line, leaving scorched corpses in its wake.

Her eyes glowed bright, unnatural. Hungry.

"I'm just getting warmed up," she whispered.

And then... came the light.

Soft at first. Gentle. Like a candle fighting against fog.

But it grew, into a radiance that pushed the darkness aside, making even the knight's armor shimmer with gold.

A final figure emerged. A woman dressed in flowing white robes, untouched by dirt or blood. Her beauty was otherworldly, skin glowing faintly, her long hair caught in a breeze that didn't exist. She held a tall staff carved from alabaster and gold, and her eyes burned not with rage, but purpose.

She lifted her staff skyward, and a golden ring of symbols ignited in the air above her. They spun faster and faster, forming a halo of power.

"By grace and flame, by soul and shield," she spoke, her voice both soft and commanding, like a lullaby cast by gods. "Protect them."

A wave of light burst out, washing over her allies.

The rogue moved faster now, his blades glowing with holy edge, wounds sealing as he danced.

The wizard's fire burned hotter, her body wreathed in protective sigils that deflected blades and arrows alike.

Even the knight, who had yet to lift his sword, now shimmered with divine protection, as if daring the world to try to break him.

The priestess stepped back, whispering blessings under her breath.

"Sanctify," she intoned, and a barrier bloomed in the air around her team.

"Heaven's Rebirth," she sang next, and a shimmering field restored wounds the moment they were made.

Then, "Judgment's Favor," and streaks of silver light rained from the sky, searing goblins where they stood.

She was not the front line, she was the soul behind it. And her power was no less deadly.

Lita pressed herself tighter against the bars, breath hitching with hope. Her heroes, no, her *saviors*, were real. Flesh and steel. Light and flame. She stared wide-eyed as goblins were torn apart by fire, shadow, and divine fury.

Then, the knight moved.

He stepped forward like an avalanche gaining momentum, each stride deliberate and crushing. The hilt of his massive sword rose from his back, and with a single fluid motion, he drew it in a wide arc, not with haste, but with weight. With *purpose.*

The goblins saw him and faltered.

They were right to.

The first one lunged, or tried to. The knight cleaved it in two from shoulder to hip with one brutal downward swing. The impact cracked the ground beneath it, a ripple of dust exploding from the force.

Another goblin rushed him from the side and was backhanded with the flat of the greatsword. Its body hit a tree with a wet crunch and didn't get back up.

He turned and swung in a brutal, horizontal arc, the sheer momentum sending three goblins flying, their weapons spinning from their hands before they even realized they'd lost limbs.

A chieftain, decorated with stolen trinkets and feathers, leapt at him with a jagged bone spear. The knight caught it midair, snapped the weapon in half with a twist of his armored hand, and slammed the hilt of his sword into the goblin's chest. Bones shattered. The goblin crumpled.

Another rushed behind him. Big mistake.

With one fluid spin, the knight reversed his grip and drove the sword backward, impaling the creature through the gut without even turning to look. He yanked it free and flicked the blood aside like it offended him.

His sword was not merely a weapon, it was a force of nature. When he swung, he parted crowds. When he stomped forward, the earth trembled.

Goblins screamed. Not in rage now, in fear. Their war cries turned into panicked screeches as they tripped over their fallen comrades trying to flee.

But there was no escape.

The knight surged forward like a black tide, carving a path through the chaos. A goblin tried to block with a rusted shield.

The sword came down and *bisected* both the shield and the goblin behind it.

He showed no emotion. No joy. No anger.

Just relentless precision.

The wizard behind him incinerated stragglers. The rogue blinked in and out of shadow, cleaning up any who slipped past. The priestess stood with her staff high, radiating a steady pulse of golden energy that shielded her allies from even the goblins' most desperate attacks.

And in the center of it all, the knight carved silence into the heart of the horde.

Lita watched with wide eyes, her breath shallow. The heroes were unstoppable. Goblins fell like wheat beneath a scythe, limbs flying, spells crashing, holy light searing through the shadows. She gripped the bars tighter, heart pounding. They were so close. Not close enough to see her yet... but they would be. Eventually.

The village was bigger than it looked from inside her cage. Crude huts formed a twisting maze of filth and debris, and beyond the burning wreckage, she knew more goblins had to be hiding, watching.

Waiting.

She hadn't seen the shamans.

Not yet.

The rogue laughed as he twirled a dagger and stepped over a twitching body.

"This is their best, huh?" he scoffed. "No wonder nobody's made it out with the Duke's daughter."

The knight smirked, wiping gore from his blade. "*Till now.*"

The wizard stood atop a mound of corpses, eyes scanning the fog for the next threat. Beside her, the priestess moved gracefully, whispering blessings as light stitched wounds closed and fatigue vanished from her allies' limbs.

And then, a sound.

Low. Rhythmic. Like drums made from wet hides and hollow bone.

From the tree line beyond the village walls, a new force emerged.

First came the frontline, larger goblins, clad in piecemeal armor made from scrap metal and reinforced bark. Their shields were massive slabs of bone lashed with sinew, and their weapons no longer looked like crude tools, but forged instruments of war.

They marched in formation, *formation,* something no goblin should've known, pounding their shields in time with the drums.

Behind them... the shamans.

A line of crooked figures swayed behind the warriors, draped in cloaks stitched from skin and feathers, their bodies painted with runes that pulsed with sickly green light. Each held a twisted staff made from blackened wood topped with shriveled animal skulls. Their eyes glowed like coals, and they began to chant.

The air grew thick.

One shaman raised his staff high, snarling something in the goblin tongue. A wave of dark mist rolled across the battlefield and hit the party like a wall.

The rogue staggered.

"Ugh, what the hell is..."

Curse of Crawling Veins.

Dark tendrils wrapped around his legs and arms, tightening like barbed wire. His speed faltered. Every movement felt like dragging weights through mud.

The knight roared and charged forward, until his vision blurred.

Curse of Hollow Eyes.

Everything twisted. He saw doubles of every goblin, illusions dancing between real threats. He struck too early, too late. His precision shattered.

The wizard lifted her hand to cast, but her fingers locked in place.

Curse of Burning Thought.

Flames licked her mind, making focus impossible. Her magic turned wild, unstable, threatening to backfire with every word she spoke.

The priestess gasped, stumbling back. A black sigil had burned itself into her chest.

Curse of the Withered Halo.

Her healing weakened, her blessings cracked at the edges. The light dimmed.

The front line of goblins slammed into the heroes in a wave of meat and rage, their shields holding firm even as the knight carved into them. They fought with more intelligence now, pairing strikes, covering one another, screaming in time with the shamans' pulse.

Lita's eyes widened.

This wasn't like before.

Her champions were no longer mowing down the enemy, they were *surviving*.

A blast of corrupted flame exploded near the wizard, throwing her back into a wall. The rogue ducked under a spear but couldn't move fast enough to avoid a second. Blood sprayed across the dirt.

The knight roared and cleaved through two shield-bearers, but his sword moved slower now, his stance less sure. The priestess raised her staff to cast a ward, but the spell fizzled as another curse wrapped around her like vines choking a rose.

The goblins had leveled up.

And they weren't done yet.

The air reeked of blood, ash, and magic gone sour.

The rogue hissed through clenched teeth, yanking a rusted goblin blade from his shoulder. "That's it. No more dancing." He flicked a vial from his belt with his pinky, cracked it on his chest, and vanished in a puff of shadow, only to reappear *inside* the goblin formation, daggers flashing in a furious storm. No more showboating. Just kill or be killed.

Every cut now cost him. His footwork faltered from blood loss, and his swings grew tighter, more desperate. He spun low, hamstrung two goblins, then ducked beneath a warhammer that would've split him in half. "Come on," he growled. "Fall *already!*"

The knight roared as he broke through a wall of shields, shoulder-checking two brutes aside before cleaving a third from hip to neck. A goblin shaman shrieked and hurled a bolt of shadow flame, and it struck his chest, denting his plate and *cracking the emblem* etched into his armor.

He grunted but didn't fall.

Instead, he turned.

And made the shaman wish *he* had.

One swing. The sword glowed gold for a blink, infused by the last of the priestess's strength, and the shaman's body burst apart like a melon struck by a cannonball.

The wizard rose from the dirt, eyes bloodshot and twitching. Magic sparked around her, barely under control. She *screamed*, not in pain but fury, and slammed her staff into the ground.

"Enough!"

A *maelstrom* of wind and embers erupted around her, forming a vortex that pulled in goblins like leaves into a bonfire. She spun, hair wild, crow circling above like a black halo.

"Frostbite Surge!" she shrieked.

A line of ice exploded from her outstretched palm, freezing an entire rank of shield-bearers mid-scream, before her staff cracked down and shattered them like brittle glass.

But she was spent. Knees buckled, fingers twitching, her magic drained down to the bone.

The priestess had no time to rest. Her chants were a frantic prayer loop now, barely holding the group together. "Holy Radiance!" she cried, waves of gold pulsing out, closing wounds that hadn't even finished bleeding. "Divine Rebuke!" A blast of white energy burst from her staff, sending a trio of goblins flying backwards.

One reached her.

Its jagged blade sank into her side.

She cried out and *still* healed the knight as he took a blow to the ribs.

They weren't fighting a battle anymore.

They were surviving a war.

And still... slowly... piece by piece...

They won.

The knight crushed the last shield goblin under his boot, sword dragging through the dirt.

The rogue stood, knees shaking, his hands covered in blood that wasn't all goblin.

The wizard leaned on her staff, smoke curling from her fingers, eyes barely able to focus.

The priestess knelt on one knee, glowing faintly, lips stained red, but still chanting, still *healing*.

The battlefield fell silent.

Smoke and corpses. Limbs. Weapons. Burned huts. Pools of black blood sizzling in the dirt.

And still... no one had found Lita.

She watched from her cage, trembling. Her heroes, bloodied and bruised, stood in the aftermath of their victory, eyes scanning the ruin for the next threat.

She pressed her hand against the cage, voice small. "I'm here..."

They didn't hear her.

Not yet.

The party stood in the wreckage, silent for a long moment. Smoke drifted between them like ghosts, curling around broken blades and twitching corpses. Their breathing was ragged. Clothes torn, armor dented, magic nearly spent. They had survived, but just barely.

The rogue was the first to crack. He let out a ragged breath, then started to laugh, wild, unfiltered. The wizard looked at him, eyes glassy, and burst into laughter too. The sound echoed across the battlefield.

"This tale will be told by bards for *years* to come," the rogue said, clutching his ribs with a crooked grin.

The priestess turned toward the knight, her eyes soft, something deeper than simple gratitude hidden in their glow. He met her gaze and smiled, his armor still dripping with blood, his sword buried halfway into the dirt beside him. They had fought side by side for countless battles... and stolen moments between.

He reached up and brushed his matted hair from his brow. "Are you well?"

She folded her hands in front of her, cheeks flushed pink. "I am," she said softly. "Thank you, Sir Knight."

His smile widened, eyes lingering on her.

Then her head *exploded.*

Blood sprayed in a wide arc, bone fragments clattering across the earth like hailstones. The rogue's laughter choked mid-breath. The wizard shrieked, stumbling back.

Standing where the priestess had just been, a towering shape now cast a long, terrible shadow across the blood-soaked ground.

An orc. Massive. Taller than any they had seen before.

Muscles coiled beneath scarred, green-gray skin. Bone armor strapped to his chest, tusks yellow with age and blood. His weapon? A tree trunk reforged into a war club, studded with jagged metal and glowing with faint, red runes.

He hadn't come through the fog.

He hadn't come through the trees.

He had been *invisible* until the moment he swung.

The knight's expression froze. His sword lifted slowly. Too slowly.

The rogue blinked, blood on his face that wasn't his.

The wizard raised her staff again, lips trembling.

And far in the distance, Lita sat in her cage.

The knight's scream was pure rage. Grief made feral. Sword raised high, he charged the orc with all the fury of a man who had just watched the light of his life turned to mist.

The rogue was right behind him, stumbling to his feet, blades flashing in both hands, blood still dripping from his nose. No plan. No strategy. Just a thirst for vengeance.

The orc turned to meet them with a cruel grin carved into his tusked face.

The knight struck first. His blade arced in, aimed to cleave the brute from collar to gut, but the orc caught the sword in his bare hand. Metal shrieked as the edge bit into his palm... and stopped. The knight's eyes went wide.

The orc *twisted*.

The knight lost his grip, spun by the momentum, and barely managed to stay on his feet. The rogue darted in, slashing at the back of the orc's leg. His dagger scraped across thick hide and muscle, barely drawing blood. The orc didn't even flinch.

He kicked the rogue in the chest.

The blow launched the thief like a sack of meat, sending him tumbling across the battlefield, coughing blood. He rolled, barely upright before the orc was on him again, a shadow of muscle and rage.

The knight came back, shoulder lowered, trying to drive his whole armored weight into the orc's side. It was like ramming a wall. The impact didn't even budge the beast, and in return, the orc grabbed him.

Fingers as thick as iron bars wrapped around the knight's torso. The metal of his cuirass *groaned* under the pressure.

The rogue blinked, literally vanishing from the dirt and reappearing above the orc, one short blade raised, ready to drive it into the brute's skull.

He never got the chance.

With a roar, the orc *swung* the knight.

Like a weapon.

The armored body slammed into the airborne rogue mid-drop. The impact cracked ribs and sent both men crashing to the ground in a heap.

But the orc didn't stop.

He raised the knight again, still gripping him by the chest like a toy soldier, and began *beating the rogue to death with him.*

Each impact was a horrible *clang-thud*, metal slamming into flesh, into dirt, into bone.

The rogue screamed once.

Then never again.

Blood sprayed in arcs. Teeth scattered like dice. A dagger skittered from limp fingers. By the time the orc was done, the rogue's body was a crumpled sack of pulp and shattered limbs. One eye dangled from its socket. The other stared blankly toward the sky.

The knight gasped, *alive*, somehow, as the orc dropped him like trash. His armor was dented and torn, torn straps exposing the bruised skin beneath. He tried to crawl. Just an inch.

The orc stepped forward.

And planted a massive, calloused foot on the knight's chest.

There was a sharp *pop*, followed by a sound like a melon being crushed under a boot.

The armor caved in.

Ribs collapsed inward like broken scaffolding. A spray of blood burst from the knight's mouth as his sternum cracked and his spine snapped beneath the weight.

The wizard screamed.

Not a battle cry.

Not defiance.

A sound of pure, hopeless horror.

She ripped the mana potion from her pouch, fingers trembling as she fumbled with the cork. Her hands were slick with sweat and blood, the cork slipped once, twice, and finally came free with a wet *pop*.

She raised the potion to her lips.

The orc crossed the distance in a single, thundering step.

His hand closed around her face.

And then he *punched*.

His fist drove her head backward, shoving the entire potion, glass vial and all, down her throat.

The sound it made was a grotesque mixture of crunching glass and tearing flesh.

Her eyes bulged.

Shards punched through the back of her neck, ripping out like crimson shrapnel. Blood and glittering slivers sprayed the ground behind her in a fan.

She twitched.

Choked.

And fell.

The battlefield became silent.

Three corpses.

One monster.

And, far in the distance, Lita watched from her cage. Her lip trembled, her eyes dry, not because she'd run out of tears, but because her body had learned there was no point in crying anymore. Another group of so-called heroes reduced to crimson mist and shattered armor. Another false hope gone. Another night in chains.

She sat back, clutching her knees to her chest, staring at the iron bars like they held back the world. Silently, she wished someone, *anyone*, would save her from this torment.

"You have *got* to be kidding me!"

The scream shattered the quiet hum of a modest living room. A balding, heavyset man with a tangled beard and an oversized keyboard slapped both hands against his desk hard enough to shake his webcam. On his monitor, glowing in mocking red, the message blinked:

Realm of Legends Online: Your party has died. Respawn In Forehound Keep? Dungeon failed.

KnifeYouLater wheezed into his headset. "*Again?* That's the third wipe this week! This is bullsh—"

"I mean... we were *so* close," CandyCain interrupted with a whine that hit somewhere between exasperated and exhausted. Her voice came crackling over the voice chat, coated in frustration and just a hint of mascara-rage.

StanBigPoppa, their knight, jumped in. "Candy, what the hell was that? You started *looting* instead of drinking your damn mana potion!"

"I didn't *start* looting, Stan," Candy snapped. "I was just checking the shaman for loot while I backed up. Don't blame *me* because you stood there like a doofus and got used like a bat on our meat piñata rogue."

An exasperated sigh drifted through the speakers.

IHealYouLongTime chimed in. "Baby, you let me *die!*"

"Okay, now hold up," Stan said, his voice softening. "I had no idea the orc was there. I didn't even have time to *taunt!* I was *doing my job!*"

"Oh, please," Knife grunted, grabbing a nearby can of soda and cracking it open so violently it fizzed all over his hand. "Your job apparently involves making out with the floor every fight. While the boss beats me to a pulp. At least this time you were a part of the fight. Unfortunately it was as the boss's weapon."

A brief, awkward silence.

"Look..." KnifeYouLater continued, voice calmer now, "we need a real strat. Something that's not 'Hope the knight tanks and Candy doesn't squirrel out for loot mid-fight.'"

"Oh I'm *sorry* I got excited!" CandyCain shot back. "You think I *like* watching us die in HD while Stan becomes a punching bag and the wizard gets force-fed a glass smoothie?"

IHealYouLongTime said, giggling despite herself, "It was kinda funny. Horrifying, but funny."

StanBigPoppa groaned. "Guys. Focus. We need to do this again. I say tomorrow night, same time. But this time, we *plan*. We get potions *before* the boss. We mark the shamans. And Candy... just don't touch anything unless it's trying to kill you, okay?"

A long silence stretched across the voice chat.

Finally, CandyCain sighed. "Yeah, yeah. But I'm starving. We've been grinding this dungeon for like, what, four hours now? My legs are asleep and my cat keeps trying to sit on my keyboard."

With a click, her name faded from the party list.

CandyCain has left the voice chat.

"Yeah, I should probably go too," said IHealYouLongTime. "I need to spend some actual quality time with my boyfriend... and maybe cry in the shower over that death. Goodnight, team."

IHealYouLongTime has left the voice chat.

"Alright," KnifeYouLater muttered. "Guess I'll go watch anime and question my life choices."

A beat passed.

"Stan?"

"I'll be on tomorrow," Stan said, voice tired. "I'm not letting that orc win again. Not this time."

"Damn right," Knife said with a grin, reaching for a half-finished bag of chips.

KnifeYouLater has left the voice chat.

Stan sat in the glow of his monitor, eyes on the loading screen of *Realm of Legends*. His character lay broken, splattered in the mud of that brutal dungeon. The priestess's blood still coated his sword. He leaned back, cracked his neck, and sighed.

"Tomorrow," he whispered. "You're going down, big guy."

With one final click, the screen dimmed, and silence returned to his darkened room.

StanBigPoppa has left the voice chat.

And back in that blood-soaked fantasy world, in a rusted iron cage tucked in the shadows of a ruined village...

Lita waited.

Still hoping.

Still watching.

Still alone.

But not forgotten.

Not yet.

The beat of the drums returned, slow at first, like the heartbeat of the cursed village itself, but with each pounding rhythm, more goblins emerged from their hovels. Shadows peeled from the mist, chittering and snarling, brandishing crude weapons and shields made of bone, rusted metal, and skin too fresh to question.

The fires flickered to life again. As if the world itself had rehearsed this torment before. The cycle beginning anew.

Lita pressed against the bars of her cage, heart racing. Her filthy hair clung to her face, streaked with blood and soot, but her eyes, those pale blue eyes, sparkled.

Someone was here.

Figures stepped through the fog. One by one.

First came a woman wrapped in flowing dark robes embroidered with glowing silver runes. Her hands glowed faintly with violet magic, and a tiny creature with dragonfly wings buzzed angrily on her shoulder. She whispered something under her breath, and the mist recoiled from her like smoke caught in reverse.

Next came a massive figure clad in blackened steel armor etched with runes. His helmet was crowned with horns, and his sword was wider than most men's torsos. His footsteps crushed the bones scattered along the path, and he walked without fear.

Then a slender, leather-clad figure slipped through the haze behind them, twirling twin daggers that gleamed unnaturally even in the shadowed gloom. She had a grin like a shark's and eyes that gleamed with anticipation. A belt full of vials clinked as she walked, and she sniffed the air like she could smell blood waiting.

Behind her came a small, hunched figure with wide goggles and a metal backpack sputtering steam. Sparks danced at his fingertips. He muttered to himself as he walked, adjusting knobs and checking tubes, looking less like a warrior and more like an inventor who had accidentally wandered into the apocalypse.

And last came a woman in golden armor that shimmered like it had never known blood. She walked with purpose, eyes locked forward, gripping a staff that pulsed with divine energy. Her lips moved in prayer, but her expression was one of stone.

Lita's breath caught in her throat.

Another party.

Could this be the one?

She wanted to scream. Wanted to call out. But she didn't. Not yet.

Not until she saw if they would live longer than the last.

The drums grew louder.

And the goblins started to charge.

Her grip tightened on the rusted bars.

Let the game begin...

FOURTEEN

THE SHELF OF MANY WORLDS

Steve sat alone, eyes lowered to the familiar matte book in his hands. Its cover was powerful, a figure loomed as it moved from a burning city. Beautiful, intriguing.

He was in his thirties now, not old, not young, just... suspended. Drifting in that vague stretch of life where people start measuring themselves by what they *haven't* done. Some might say he'd wasted his years. He was soft around the edges, hair thinning, and the idea of romance had always been more theoretical than personal. Real connection had somehow passed him by.

But he had this.

He lifted his gaze and looked around the room. Shelves lined every wall, sagging under the weight of paper worlds. His sanctuary. His kingdom.

Or maybe... *these.*

Books.

There was something sacred about a good book, the way it lured your mind away from fluorescent lights and rent notices into lands of sword and sorcery, into moments so vivid you could *smell* the fire, *feel* the danger, *ache* with the hero. Steve sighed quietly, the sound swallowed by the room's silence. He wished, truly wished, there was magic in *this* world. Real magic. The kind you could summon. The kind that made you *matter*.

Maybe then... maybe *then*, he'd feel like someone special.

He turned the book in his hands, eyes falling to the worn cover like they always did.

The Book of Devaultus.

He'd read it more times than he could count. One of many stories that didn't just entertain, they *consumed*. Pulled him through the page and made him the hero. The assassin. The sorcerer. The deceiver. In these books, he *was* someone. *Important*. He loved that feeling, that surge of belonging, the thrill of pretending he wasn't just Steve-from-nowhere, but a legend waiting to be awakened.

Steve sipped his morning coffee and lifted the book. As always, the world around him began to blur, his drab apartment dissolving into mist and memory. Reality *swirled*, colors smeared like oil in water and then shifted.

He was looking down at himself.

A balding, pudgy cook bustled about a busy tavern kitchen, sweat dotting his brow as he rushed to plate steaming dishes. The scent in the air was intoxicating, seared meat, baked bread, spices that tickled the back of his throat. He could almost *taste* it.

Yes. He was here again.

In the world.

The tavern beyond the swinging door echoed with laughter and sloshing tankards. Patrons bellowed toasts in his name, praising the chef who had turned a humble meal into a night worth remembering. The bar wenches, all curves and cheer, bounced between tables, grinning wide when they caught sight of him. One winked. Another blew a kiss.

It was... *good*.

Not easy, no, tavern life never was, but here, he was *seen*. Appreciated. The stink of travel-weary adventurers filled the room like an invisible fog, rank and heavy, but he didn't mind it. That smell meant people. *His* people. They came here for a warm meal, safety, and a taste of magic. And he got to give it to them.

Then...

Ding-dong.

The sound sliced through the fantasy like a blade through silk.

Steve blinked.

The tavern vanished. The scent of roasted duck turned into cold coffee. The laughter faded, replaced by the dull hum of his refrigerator. He sat in his apartment once again; book open in his lap.

The doorbell rang again.

Frowning, he placed a bookmark carefully between the pages and rose to his feet, stretching out stiff limbs as he padded toward the door. He wasn't expecting anyone. Who rang doorbells this early, anyway?

Peering through the peephole, he blinked in surprise.

It was Cara, one of his neighbors.

She was a petite redhead with glasses perched on her nose and a wardrobe that leaned delightfully into the nerdy side of fashion, oversized sweaters with pixelated dragons, comic book socks, the occasional cape on Halloween. She looked up at the door expectantly, shifting her weight like someone rehearsing a line in their head.

Cara shifted her weight from one hip to the other, fidgeting with the sleeve of her sweater.

"Uhm... hello, Steve," she said, her voice soft, eyes darting up at him before quickly looking away.

He blinked. "Hey, Cara."

A pause. She pushed her glasses up the bridge of her nose, clearly nervous.

"So, listen... I finished Book One of *Chains of the Withered Realm,* and, well..." She glanced toward his window. "I've noticed your library from across the way. My room's just across from yours. You see..."

She trailed off, cheeks flushing with color.

"I was just wondering if you... by chance, have Book Two?" she asked, almost apologetically.

Steve stared at her for a second, caught completely off guard. Then he nodded, rubbing the back of his neck.

"Uhm... yeah. Yeah, I do. Come on in," he said, stepping aside.

Cara entered cautiously as Steve led the way through the small apartment. It was lived-in but clean, decorated with posters of towering Amazonian warriors, shelves of superhero action figures, and a large, lovingly maintained fish tank glowing faintly in the corner.

And then... the *library.*

An entire wall, floor to ceiling, packed with books. Rows upon rows. *Fantasy, LitRPGs, short stories, comics,* a shrine to every genre imaginable. Cara stepped toward it, eyes wide. Her fingers drifted along the spines as if they were made of gold.

"They're beautiful," she murmured. *Each one contains a world of its own,* she thought to herself.

Steve smiled quietly, searching through a nearby shelf.

Of course, he thought they were beautiful. But he wouldn't tell her that. He didn't want her to think he was weird or anything.

After a moment, he found the one he was looking for, *Chains of the Withered Realm: Book Two.* He slid it free and turned.

"Here it is," he said, holding it out.

She took it gently, like it was something precious. The spine was worn, the pages slightly yellowed, but she didn't seem to mind. In fact, she smiled. *Really* smiled.

"I think I can finish it by next week," she said.

Steve nodded. "Cool. I've got the rest of the series too, if you want them after."

She looked up at him, the faintest blush on her cheeks. "Okay. Thank you."

He walked her to the door, opening it for her. Pausing in the doorway, book in hand.

"Well... I guess I'll see you in a week," she said.

"Okay," he replied, giving a little wave. "Goodbye."

He closed the door gently behind her but didn't move away. Instead, he leaned toward the peephole, watching.

Cara lingered outside for a moment, staring at the door, holding the book against her chest. Then she turned and walked down the hall.

Steve exhaled and leaned back.

He'd watched her before, walking down the street, chatting with neighbors, laughing at some joke. He'd thought, *What a beautiful girl. Why can't I meet someone like her?*

And now she'd stood right here.

But the thought crept in, quiet and cruel.

She'd never be interested in a guy like you, Steve.

With a sigh, he turned away from the door and returned to his seat. The book still sat where he'd left it, pages open, waiting.

Waiting to take his mind to a place where he mattered.

Steve sat back down, his eyes falling once more to the open book. He exhaled a soft breath, heart still carrying the weight of her smile, the echo of her voice.

"Now then," he murmured to himself, brushing his fingers across the page. "Back to you."

He wished he was confident. Like the people in these stories. Bold. Certain. Important.

He opened the book, ready to fall back into his adventure.

Knock knock.

Steve froze.

Again?

"Did she forget something?" he muttered, setting the book down once more. He stood and walked toward the door, already picturing Cara's flustered expression, maybe a half-laugh as she realized she'd dropped her bookmark or left her phone.

But when he peered through the peephole...

There was *no one* there.

Frowning, he opened the door and stepped into the hallway. Empty. Silent. Even the air felt still.

"That's... odd," he said aloud, glancing left and right. "Maybe someone knocked on the wrong door."

He turned back toward the apartment.

Knock knock.

He stopped cold.

The sound had come again. Loud. Close. *Intentional.*

He spun back around and flung the door open, ready to catch the prankster in the act.

Instead, he found someone sitting on the floor just outside his doorway.

It was an elderly man.

Steve looked up and down the hallway. No one else. Just the old man, hunched slightly, skin mottled with age spots, his hands twisted with time and sun. He wore an old, thin, ragged coat and resting on his head was a hat. It's brim long and flopping.

"Are you alright, sir?" Steve asked, startled. He shifted uncertainly. What the hell was he supposed to do here?

The man looked up at him, blinking slowly. His eyes were pale and watery, but sharp behind the haze.

"Hello, lad," the man said, voice rasping like sandpaper. "I daresay I've had too much sun today. Could I trouble you for a glass of water?"

Steve hesitated.

He knew better than to let strangers into his home. He really did. But the man looked like he could barely stand. Frail. Lost. And there was something familiar in the way he spoke, something warm, almost... literary.

"Okay," Steve said, stepping forward. "Come in. Have a seat."

The man tried to rise but faltered twice, legs trembling beneath him. Steve reached down and gently helped him to his feet, guiding him inside and over to the small dining table. The old man sat with a grateful sigh.

Steve crossed into the kitchen, filled a glass with water, and placed it in front of him.

The old man smiled, his lips thin and cracked. "Thank you, lad. I don't know what I would've done if I hadn't found your place."

Steve tilted his head slightly. That was strange. There were half a dozen apartments on this floor. The paper-thin walls rarely left people's business their own. He was sure he would have heard him earlier. It seemed the man had passed every single one... just to knock on his.

The old man let out a long sigh as he drank the water, each sip slow and deliberate. Steve watched for a moment, then stepped forward to pick up the empty glass. He turned and walked to the sink, rinsing it absently before filling it again.

When he turned back, the man was gone.

Steve blinked.

The chair was empty.

Frowning, he set the refilled glass on the table and scanned the apartment. The door was still closed. No sound. No sign of footsteps.

Then, movement. In the office.

Steve crept forward, cautious now, unsure whether to be worried or just confused. The old man stood in front of the bookshelves, hands folded behind his back like a professor in a private archive, eyes slowly roaming over the spines. His posture was straighter than before. More stable. How had he moved so quickly?

Steve hesitated, casting a glance toward his phone on the counter. *Should I be calling someone?*

The old man reached out a trembling hand and gently touched one of the books, *The Martian Chronicles*. His calloused fingers traced the worn spine with reverence.

"You like to read?" the man asked softly, his voice barely above a whisper.

Steve nodded instinctively, then realized the man wasn't looking at him.

"Yes, sir," he replied, stepping a bit closer.

The man moved slowly to another shelf, examining the titles with an almost fatherly fondness.

"Have you read all of these?" he asked.

Steve scratched the back of his neck. "Yes, sir. Every one of them. Most of them more than once."

The old man smiled faintly, a private smile meant for no one but himself.

"And why?" he asked. "Why do you enjoy them so much?"

Steve stepped beside him. The man was gazing at a leather-bound volume nestled near the middle of the shelf. Steve reached out and pulled it free, brushing a thumb across the faded title.

"Because they have these... wonderful worlds," Steve said quietly. "Places where anything can happen. Where the rules are different. Where people *matter*."

He looked down at the book in his hands, the corners of his mouth curling into something soft. Almost a smile. He held it as if it were a memory he didn't want to lose.

The old man nodded slowly.

"So, you mean there's something in those books," the old man asked, "that you can't find here?"

Steve smiled faintly to himself. "Yes," he said, with rare certainty. "Exactly that."

The old man scratched his head, brow furrowing in thought. "And what, may I ask, is in them?"

Steve looked down at the book in his hands again, his thumb brushing the worn cover.

"This one's about a dark elf," he began, voice soft. "He's an outcast. Alone. Then he meets this group of people, strange, broken, brilliant people, and together, they face down the worst this world throws at them. He becomes a hero. They love him. They treat him like he matters. Like he's *somebody.*"

His eyes lingered on the cover, full of quiet longing.

The old man chuckled gently, then reached for another book, plucking it from the shelf with slow, deliberate hands.

"This one? What is it, *Realm of Legends Online*?"

Steve looked over. "That one's about a guy who's a nobody in real life. Gets pushed around, overlooked. Bullied. But he gets pulled into a virtual world, and there, he becomes something more. A warrior. A legend. Someone people cheer for."

The old man nodded thoughtfully, tapping the cover.

"And do you believe," he asked, "that's something you *can't* have in this world?"

Steve laughed, but there was no joy in it. Just a quiet ache.

"Of course not," he said, shrugging. "There's no magic here. Nothing to make someone like *me* a hero."

His voice cracked a little on the last word. Somber. Small.

The old man watched him for a long moment. Silent.

Then, slowly, he placed the book back on the shelf, straightened it, and said:

"Oh, lad." Gently, he continued, "that's where you're wrong. This world has *plenty* of magic."

Steve let out a bitter laugh. "Oh really? And what?" His voice sharpened, a coldness in his tone now, "You gonna teach me spells? Show me how to shoot fireballs from my hands?"

It wasn't a joke. Not really. He sounded like a man who felt mocked by hope.

But the old man just smiled. Not smugly. Kindly. Like someone who understood that pain all too well.

"I don't need to teach you anything," he said softly. "You *already know* magic, my boy."

Steve scoffed, shaking his head. "Do I? I mean, I cook a mean stir-fry, but that's about the closest I've ever come to conjuring something special."

The man chuckled, then reached over and gently took the book from Steve's hands.

"This one," he said, turning it in his fingers. "The dark elf story. Did you realize he starts off as a nobody? Alone. Hopeless. No friends. No future. And what changed?"

Steve frowned, thinking.

The old man held the book like it was holy.

"He made a *choice*," he said. "He got tired of being no one. He left the underworld. He stirred the pot. He *forced* himself to become something more."

He turned and slid the book carefully back onto the shelf.

"Do you think," he continued, "he'd have been a hero if he stayed underground? Quiet? Afraid of the world?"

Steve shook his head slowly. "No... I suppose not."

The old man nodded, then pointed to another book. *Realm of Legends Online.*

"And this one? What if he got pulled into the game world, found a hut... and just stayed there? Didn't fight. Didn't risk anything. Just sat and waited for something to happen."

Steve stared at the cover, then spoke without looking up.

"He'd be exactly who he was before. Nothing would change."

The old man grinned. "Correct. Every one of those characters believed their worlds had no magic either. At least, no magic for them. Until they *chose* to do something extraordinary."

He turned to face Steve fully now, eyes bright beneath his weathered brow.

"The only people who can use magic in this world... are the ones who create it *themselves*."

The old man reached down and picked up the book Steve had been reading.

"Ahh... this one's something new, isn't it?" he said, turning it over in his gnarled hands. "What's it about?"

Steve scratched his chin, thinking.

"I haven't gotten far yet," he admitted. "But it's about a man who's lost everything. Everyone. He doesn't want to be a hero."

The old man looked up sharply. "And why do you think that is?"

Steve hesitated. "I... I'm not sure. Maybe because being a hero means responsibility. Maybe because he doesn't think the world *deserves* to be saved. Maybe he's heartbroken. Too much loss, too much pain. I honestly haven't read enough to know."

The old man smiled gently, almost knowingly.

"Ahh... so you have a man with the *power* to act, but not the *will*. He could change things. But he doesn't. Because he thinks caring only leads to pain. He thinks fighting for something only guarantees heartbreak."

He looked up at Steve, eyes gleaming beneath his tired lids.

"Maybe this story has a bit more to do with *you* than you thought."

Steve blinked, as the old man picked up the book, holding it as if it had just lightened in his hands.

"What do you mean?" he asked.

The old man's smile deepened, not mocking, but full of quiet truth.

"You hide in here," he said softly. "You dream of a magical world. You fill your shelves with heroes and dragons, with kingdoms and quests, because here, you're safe. In here, *nothing* can hurt you."

He paused.

"But if you *left* this little world? If you made friends, and they left you...? If you met a maiden... and she didn't want you...?" His voice softened. "You're afraid you wouldn't survive it."

Steve said nothing.

The old man placed the book gently on the table, as if returning a sacred object.

"There *is* magic in this world, lad," he said with a chuckle. "Every single one of these books, they were written *here*. On this Earth. By people who were scared, just like you. People who dared to hope. They crafted entire universes using nothing but ink, paper, and pain. That's magic of the mind."

He looked around the room, at the towering library.

"Sure, you can live in those worlds," he said. "You can close your eyes and imagine them. You can pretend you're someone else for a while. But all the while, you'll be missing the one magic these books can't give you."

Steve looked up slowly.

"What magic is that?" he asked.

The old man's smile changed to a wistful look.

"The kind you live."

He turned then, walked slowly toward the door.

"But I have a feeling," the old man added, hand resting on the door handle, "that there's *a lot* of magic in you."

He turned slightly, giving Steve a warm, knowing smile.

"Enjoy the many worlds you've collected, Steve. Just don't *live* in them. You have a world around you that *needs* your magic."

He paused, eyes twinkling.

"By the way... that book you're holding?" He nodded toward it. "It's one of my favorites."

Then, without waiting for a reply, he stepped through the doorway and made his way down the hall, his steps slow but certain.

Steve watched him go, confusion and awe battling across his face. He looked down at the book in his hands, the one the old man had been holding, and noticed something lying on top of it.

A pencil.

Oddly shaped. Intricate. Carved with swirling symbols that didn't seem like anything he'd ever seen. Definitely not something you found at an office supply store.

Must've been the old man's.

Steve picked it up carefully, then returned his attention to the book. He flipped it over, scanning the back cover out of curiosity.

There, in the *About the Author* section...

His heart stopped.

It was him.

The old man. Smiling from a black-and-white author photo like he had *every right* to be there.

Steve shot to his feet, adrenaline flooding his veins. He rushed to the door, yanked it open, and stepped into the hall, but the corridor was empty. Dead silent. Not even the echo of footsteps.

He stood there for a moment, stunned. Mouth dry. Mind racing.

Did I really just have the author of this book... in my apartment?

Slowly, he closed the door and walked back inside, dazed. He sat down, picked up the book, and opened the cover.

There, in thick, looping script just beneath the title page, was a handwritten note:

Steve, I look forward to living in your magical world someday.

You have magic. Now don't be afraid to use it.
You're welcome.

Steve stared at the message, his heart pounding.

When had he written that?

He hadn't taken his eyes off the man for more than a second.

And more importantly...

How did he know Steve's name?

Steve sat in silence for a long moment, the old man's words echoing through his mind like the last notes of a song that refused to fade.

He looked down at the strange pencil, turning it over in his fingers. The carvings glinted faintly under the light, the symbols unfamiliar but... comforting. A quiet part of him wondered, had *this very pencil written the story he was holding?* It seemed impossible.

But maybe, just maybe, he'd believe it anyway.

He tucked the pencil gently into his pocket and stood up.

Crossing the room, he paused at the door, his hand resting on the knob.

That man in *Realm of Legends Online*... What would've happened if he had found a hut in that game and *never left it*?

Steve stared at the door.

He wouldn't stay in his hut any longer.

He would find his own magic.

He turned the knob, opened it wide, and stepped out into a world brimming with possibilities.

His feet carried him down the hall.

Straight to *Cara's* door.

And he knocked.

Down the hall, the old man stood in shadow, watching.

A wide, toothy grin spread beneath the brim of his weathered hat.

"Atta boy, Steve," he whispered to himself. "It's dangerous out there... but have no doubt, you'll find your magic. And you'll make this world yours."

With that, he tipped the hat.

And vanished into the dark hallway.

Fifteen

Once Upon a Breath

The day stretched out before Kayla like a dream, breathtaking in its simple perfection. The sun hung low enough in the sky to cast a warm, honeyed light that caressed her skin with tender fingers. She lifted her hand slowly, almost reverently, and let the gentle heat seep into her palm, a soft balm that seemed to pulse with the quiet heartbeat of the earth itself.

Her eyes fluttered closed for a moment, savoring the sensation, before she blinked them open just in time to see a delicate butterfly drift down from the shimmering canopy above. It settled softly on her outstretched fingers, its wings folding and unfolding like fragile tissue paper.

"Hello, little butterfly," Kayla whispered, her voice a melody in the still air, a smile curving her lips like the first rays of dawn. The butterfly remained still, as if understanding the kindness in her tone, and she felt a tender connection, a small significant bridge between her mind and nature.

Around her, the world breathed in hushed rhythms. The stillness was not empty, but alive, the subtle rustling of leaves, the faint hum of distant bees working their magic, and the whisper of the breeze threading through the branches. Here, the burdens of the world felt far away, replaced by a serene peace that wrapped around her like a soft blanket.

From the corner of her eye, Kayla noticed a squirrel perched on a nearby tree trunk, its small frame tense with cautious curiosity. The creature's bright eyes flicked to her, twitching whiskers betraying its intrigue. For a moment, the two regarded each other silently, bound by a shared moment of quiet wonder in a world that often rushed too fast to notice such simple beauty.

Kayla lifted her hand from the small butterfly with a sigh of contentment, brushing a few stray strands of her dark hair away from her face. The sunlight caught the glossy waves, making them shimmer in the golden light. She walked slowly to her vehicle, each step soft on the forest floor, careful not to disturb the delicate harmony around her.

From inside, she retrieved a small bottle of water, the coolness of it refreshing in the warmth, and a handful of mixed nuts she had packed earlier, almonds, walnuts, and a few pecans, their earthy scent mingling with the fresh pine and moss in the air. With practiced ease, she crouched down on the soft earth, careful not to startle the woodland creatures, and scattered the nuts gently onto the ground.

Extending her hand, palm open and steady, Kayla waited patiently. At first, the squirrel watched from the safety of a nearby branch, its bright eyes wide and twitching with cautious curiosity. Then slowly, emboldened by her calm presence, it hopped down, tiny paws barely making a sound as it approached. The little creature delicately took a few nuts directly from her palm, its soft fur, brushing against her fingers, warm and surprisingly gentle.

"Well, aren't you a cute little thing," Kayla said softly, her smile growing wider as the squirrel nibbled contentedly, its whiskers twitching with delight.

Her heart swelled with quiet joy in the simple exchange, the peace of the moment settling around her like a gentle embrace.

Suddenly, a subtle rustling sound from behind broke the stillness. Kayla turned slowly, every movement deliberate and calm, as if bracing for something unexpected to leap from the shadows. But the forest remained serene, the sunlight filtering through the leaves in lazy, golden shafts.

Her gaze settled on a baby deer peeking shyly through the brush. The fawn's large, dark eyes reflected the dappled light, full of cautious wonder. It stepped forward tentatively, as if unsure whether this human might be a friend, or a predator out to find its dinner.

The fawn stepped forward with the lightest touch, each delicate hoof-fall nearly silent on the soft forest floor. Its movements were slow and cautious, as if it were testing the safety of this quiet clearing where the squirrel had found such an unexpected feast. The gentle rustle of leaves whispered beneath its slender legs, while its large, expressive eyes flicked nervously from the nut-strewn ground to Kayla's calm figure.

Sniffing the air with tentative curiosity, the fawn lowered its velvety nose toward the scattered treats. Its breath came soft and warm, mingling with the earthy scent of pine needles and rich soil. Slowly, it reached down and took a few of the leftover nuts between its lips, nibbling them gently with the delicate precision of a creature accustomed to tenderness.

Kayla held her breath, her heart swelling with a quiet warmth as she watched the small, fragile creature accept her offering. Time seemed to slow, the forest holding its breath alongside her in this fragile moment of trust.

With a careful, almost reverent motion, she extended her hand toward the fawn, inviting it closer. For a heartbeat, the fawn hesitated, its large eyes wide with uncertainty. It took a tentative step back, as if weighing the risk of this strange yet kind presence.

But the scent of the treats, the promise of kindness, proved too tempting to resist. Slowly, almost shyly, the fawn edged forward once more, the fragile thread of trust beginning to weave itself between human and nature in this sunlit glade.

When the fawn finally stepped close enough, Kayla reached out slowly, her fingers trembling with quiet excitement. She let her hand glide gently through the soft, velvety fur along the creature's slender neck, marveling at the delicate warmth beneath her touch. The fawn flinched ever so slightly, a flash of uncertainty, before it relaxed completely, surrendering to the comfort of her presence as it continued nibbling on the scattered nuts.

A soft giggle bubbled up through Kayla's lips as the fawn's rough, warm tongue unexpectedly flicked across her hand. The sensation was startling yet sweet, a tender reminder of the delicate life she was touching. The fawn's ears twitched, swiveling toward the deeper shadows of the forest, alert and watchful for any sudden sounds.

Just then, a small rustle from the underbrush caught Kayla's attention. From the dense greenery emerged a curious rabbit, its nose twitching rapidly as it hopped closer with cautious steps. Its bright eyes reflected a mixture of wonder and hunger, drawn by the promise of the treats.

The rabbit's curiosity matched the fawn's as it approached Kayla's outstretched hand, which she had quietly refilled with another small handful of the tasty offering. The gentle creature paused only briefly before delicately taking a few morsels, its tiny paws pressing softly against her skin.

"Well, aren't I just popular," Kayla said with a soft laugh, her smile brightening as her eyes sparkled with genuine delight. The joy of being surrounded by these curious little creatures filled her with a warmth that radiated from her chest like gentle sunlight.

The rabbit nibbled eagerly at the treats in her hand, its tiny teeth working quickly as it savored the taste. Then, almost bursting with excitement, it bounced up and down in place, its fluffy tail twitching like a little metronome keeping time with its happy heart.

Caught up in the playful spirit, the fawn began to hop too, matching the rabbit's joyful leaps with clumsy but enthusiastic bounds. The two animals seemed to share a secret language, a game only they could understand, a dance of innocence and delight beneath the swaying branches.

Nearby, the squirrel, perched on a low branch with its bushy tail flicking in irritation, let out a sharp chittering protest. Its voice was firm, a scolding reminder that the feast was its own, yet even in its grumbling there was a hint of reluctant amusement. Despite the squirrel's objections, the woodland trio continued their gentle dance, fur brushing against fur as they played and leapt in carefree abandon.

Now and then, the creatures paused to sip from a small puddle of water Kayla had left nearby or to nibble at fresh handfuls of treats she offered with tender hands. The clearing was filled with soft sounds of excitement from the creatures, as well as rustling leaves, and happy chitters, a perfect moment of harmony woven into the fabric of the forest.

Kayla's warm brown eyes drifted from one creature to the next, her gaze tender and filled with wonder. The sunlight spilled through the tree canopy, warm and inviting, catching on the soft fur of the fawn nestled beside her and the playful scampering of a squirrel darting up the bark of a towering oak. She turned slowly, arms outstretched, and her sundress swirled around her legs like a cloud spun from morning dew.

She began to hum, a delicate, melodic tune that seemed to come from some long-forgotten part of herself. It danced through the forest, brushing the leaves, curling through the air like the laughter of ghosts. Birds flitted around her, chirping brightly, caught in the current of her voice. Butterflies spiraled upward like living confetti.

This was happiness. Real, pure, unfiltered joy. Her smile widened as she glanced around. The sun warmed her cheeks. The breeze tickled her hair. Everything was as it should have been.

Then she noticed the fawn.

It stood still, its eyes fixed ahead. The edges of its form began to shimmer. A flicker. Then another. Kayla tilted her head, curiosity slowly pulling her from the moment. She reached toward it, and the squirrel vanished in a static blur. Like a broken signal.

Her breath caught.

One by one, the animals dissolved into distortion, their shapes flickering, pixelating, then blinking out of existence. The trees followed. The sky fractured. The song in her throat died.

All that remained was the cold hum of technology.

Before her stood a tall man, clad in a sterile military suit. The forest was now completely gone, the walls around her gleamed with silver paneling, and the scent of real earth was replaced by recycled air and sterilized metal.

He stood at attention and saluted. "Lieutenant Kayla White. You are needed on the bridge."

Kayla sighed and rubbed her temples, a twinge of frustration clouding her expression. The brief illusion of peace was gone, snatched away like a dream at the alarm bell. "At ease," she said, brushing past him.

He dropped his salute. "Yes, ma'am."

"What's your name, soldier?" she asked while gathering her belongings, a slim pack, her datapad, the regulation jacket with its crisp insignia.

He hesitated. "Ma'am?"

She turned, leveling him with a look. "Name. You've got one, don't you?"

He straightened. "Private Nicholas Stern, ma'am."

She gave a short nod and walked toward the sliding door, boots echoing in the sterile hallway. Private Stern followed in step.

They passed through corridor after corridor of smooth gray walls and flickering light strips. Even with hundreds of crew members aboard, it always felt empty here, too quiet, too clean.

Kayla glanced over at him. "That really how it was?" she asked, her voice carrying a note of melancholy. "Records show it's the most-used simulation on the ship. I've never seen anything like it."

He glanced at her, uncertain. "Permission to speak freely?"

She let out a soft exhale. "Go ahead, Private. Just two friends talking."

He scratched the back of his neck. "Well, ma'am... the holo-program pulls from all known video, text, and cultural records of Earth, from back before we stripped it bare. Before the forests died and the animals followed."

Kayla said nothing.

"Though..." he added with a sheepish look, "after a few hundred years, I guess it's safe to say the files might not be exact. Some things... might be a little too perfect."

Kayla didn't respond right away. As they walked, she reached up and ran her fingers along one of the synthetic vines snaking down the wall, part of the "aesthetic upgrade" the crew was supposed to appreciate. It had the *shape* of life, but none of its soul. The leaves felt like wax. The stems were stiff, too clean, too sterile.

Even the air here was wrong. It carried the sharp tang of purifiers and ozone, layered beneath the faint metallic undertone of industrial filters. Food tasted like chalk with hints of vitamin. Showers smelled like disinfectant. Life, such as it was, had been boiled down to calories, chemicals, and schedule rotations.

She followed the Private in silence until the massive doors to the bridge whooshed open with a mechanical hiss.

Inside, a dozen high-ranking officers stood around the central holo-table, their attention snapping toward her. That many brass in one place was never a good sign.

One of them, a stern-faced man with silver in his hair and deep lines across his brow, stepped forward. "Lieutenant Kayla White?"

"Sir," she replied, standing to attention.

He gave a short nod. "At 2100 yesterday, one of our long-range scout drones made contact with a planet. Preliminary readings show it possesses an atmospheric and molecular structure nearly identical to Earth's... before the collapse."

Kayla's heart gave a small, startled jolt.

"We've yet to make planetfall, but we want you to assemble a team and prepare for surface scouting." His expression was grave, but hopeful. "I don't need to tell you how important this mission is, do I, Lieutenant?"

She straightened, voice calm. "No, sir. I understand. I'll leave in ten."

Without waiting for a dismissal, she flipped on her comm unit. "Bravo Two-One-Three, report to Bay Two. Expedition Protocol Three-One-Four-Five is in effect."

The commander gave her a rare smile. "Dismissed."

Kayla turned sharply and exited, heels clicking with purpose. As she strode toward the equipment lockers, her pulse quickened, not from nerves, but from possibility. She suited up swiftly, pulling on her military uniform with practiced ease, strapping on her weapon belt and shoulder pack.

Her team was already assembling in the hangar, each soldier moving with the energy of a child told they were going outside to play for the first time.

She couldn't blame them. She felt the same way.

The crew descended through the upper layers of the planet's atmosphere, their shuttle slicing through the clouds like a silent predator. A soft vibration hummed through the cabin as the ship adjusted to the wind currents below. Inside, faces pressed against reinforced glass, eyes wide with awe.

Below them stretched an untouched world, verdant, wild, and breathtaking. It wasn't just habitable... it was *beautiful*. Towering trees draped in vines stood like silent giants. Rivers shimmered with a crystalline glow. Great open plains seemed to wave to them as the breeze blew the many blades of grass. It looked less like a planet and more like a forgotten paradise pulled straight from the archives of old Earth fairy-tales.

Sensors had swept the surface and returned clean: no human life. No intelligent lifeforms at all, at least not anything that responded to scans. Just a thriving ecosystem teeming with animal life, lush flora, and curious terrain. That last part was what interested Kayla most.

The rear ramp of the ship groaned open with a hiss, and Lieutenant Kayla White led the way. Her boots touched down on fresh, living soil that hadn't felt the weight of a single step in countless years, if ever. Her team followed, moving with military precision, helmets filtering the atmosphere as their systems cross-checked air quality, pollen count, microbial presence, and everything else that might kill them slowly or all at once.

None of it did. Instead, the world met them with calm birdsong and warm air, and the gentle rustle of leaves stirred by a breeze that smelled of pine and citrus. It was disorienting, too perfect. Kayla had spent her life in artificial habitats and recycled oxygen. This... this was overwhelming.

She gave a series of silent hand signals to the squad, directing them northward. Their pre-landing scans had picked up faint geometric anomalies in that direction, structures of some kind. That was unusual. No intelligent life, yet buildings? Curious.

The squad slipped through the alien forest, weapons at the ready. They moved like shadows through the underbrush, stepping over gnarled roots and ducking beneath massive ferns that unfurled like wings. Their scanners worked in tandem, cataloging everything they passed: plant life, mineral compositions, insect species... It was all logged and transmitted in real time to the ship's mainframe.

Then, the lead scout halted. A fist raised in the air.

Kayla stopped. So did everyone else.

The silence tightened like a noose. Only the chirping of distant wildlife broke the stillness.

The lead scout crouched low, hand motioning for them to spread out and advance slowly. Kayla nodded and adjusted her rifle, stepping forward with deliberate care.

Ahead, the trees began to thin. And beyond them...

Ruins.

Ancient ruins.

A clearing opened up, dotted with crumbling huts, their thatched roofs long since collapsed and walls overtaken by vines and moss. Structures made of wood, and stone, arranged in familiar shapes but undeniably alien in execution. It was a village... or had been, once.

Kayla's breath caught.

These weren't natural formations. Someone, or *something*, had lived here. Long enough to build homes, settle down... and then vanish without a trace.

And her scanners still read nothing.

No movement. No life signs. Not even a decaying energy signature.

She knelt slowly, her fingers brushing the edge of a broken stone carved with strange symbols.

They had landed on a graveyard.

The unsettling part wasn't that the buildings were falling apart, that was expected. What bothered Kayla was how none of them looked like they'd ever been lived in. Not truly. The structures were identical. Same layout, same crude furniture, same placement of every object, down to the crooked chairs and dust-covered dishes. It was as if someone had built a village from memory, or from a blueprint. And then simply walked away.

"Lieutenant!" a voice crackled over comms. "You're gonna want to see this."

Kayla bolted from the hut, boots crunching softly over moss and decaying wood. She followed the sound until she reached one of the outer cabins, where a soldier stood frozen beside a lopsided porch.

She paused the color draining from her face.

A skeleton sat in a rocking chair, hunched forward slightly as if waiting for something. Its bones were bleached by time, and the chair had a slow, gentle sway, creaking faintly in the breeze.

There was no sign of a struggle. No sign of burial or reverence. Just a chair, a porch, and a forgotten corpse that didn't match any known record from the scans.

She took a slow step forward, heart thudding in her chest. "Get me a full scan. Now."

The soldier paled visibly, even beneath his helmet. His voice crackled through the comms, tight and urgent. "We already ran the scan, ma'am. It's human."

Kayla blinked. For a moment she thought she'd misheard. "What do you mean, *human*?" she asked, stepping toward him, boots crunching lightly on the overgrown path.

The soldier turned, locking eyes with her through the visor. "I mean it's from Earth. Genetic markers match. But based on decay and bone density, the body is *centuries* old."

She looked down at the skeleton again, now seeing it differently. This wasn't some alien corpse, nor the relic of a vanished off-world colony. This was one of *theirs*. From Earth. Human. And it had been here for a long time, *too* long a time... it was here from a time before anyone from their mission had ever left orbit.

"That's impossible," she murmured. "We're the first team to travel this far. The first launch outside of Sol that wasn't just a deep probe. No recorded expeditions. No terraforming logs. No human presence."

And yet here it was. Flesh long gone, slumped comfortably in what could only be described as a rocking chair. There was something both eerie and tragically peaceful about it.

Beside the skeleton sat a book, an actual book, bound in cracked leather, browned at the edges by time. The fact it hadn't completely turned to dust was a miracle in itself.

"ChronoSeal," Kayla said sharply, extending a hand.

One of the techs jogged over, carrying a small metallic dispenser with a silver applicator. He pressed it into her hand without a word. Kayla thumbed the activation switch.

The nozzle hissed softly, releasing a nearly invisible mist that coated the surface of the book. Millions of microscopic nanobots deployed instantly, crawling across the fragile material. Each was equipped with adaptive bonding agents, engineered to weave molecular lattice supports beneath brittle fibers, stabilizing the structure without compromising readability. Within seconds, the book was preserved, readable, and safe to touch without it crumbling into powder.

Kayla knelt and picked it up with a kind of reverence usually reserved for ancient religious texts. It was heavier than she expected. Real. Tangible. Unfathomable.

"Commander," one of the science officers chimed in through her comms, "we've completed secondary atmospheric analysis. No pathogens, no toxins. Oxygen and nitrogen levels are identical to Earth's. It's safe to breathe."

"Copy that," Kayla said distantly. "Helms off, people."

One by one, the soldiers removed their helmets, each of them sucking in a breath of impossibly Earth-like air.

But Kayla didn't move. Her eyes were locked on the book in her hands. Slowly, carefully, she opened it to the first page.

The handwriting was crude but legible, clearly written with a charcoal pen.

I am Conner Artorious. Number one best explorer of all time. Ever. Period. Not that it means much these days. Explorers are a dying breed. Metaphorically, sure. But also, literally. Let me explain.

Kayla stared at the name. Her mind spun.

"Who the hell *was* Conner Artorious?" she whispered.

Behind her, the wind picked up, rattling the half-collapsed huts. The rocking chair creaked once.

Suddenly, she heard a noise behind her, sharp, desperate gasping. She spun on instinct. One of her soldiers was clutching his chest, collapsing to his knees. She turned to call for the medic, but he was already down, convulsing, his hands clawing at the air.

"Sir, what's happening?" she barked into her comms, voice tight with rising panic. "I thought the scans were cleared?"

No response.

She glanced down at her wrist scanner. The screen was black... then it blinked to life with a restart cycle.

"Now? You restart *now*?" she shouted, slamming her fist against it.

The Veldt Corp. logo flashed with a slow, pulsing loading bar. She could practically hear the smug jingle.

Her team was crumpling one by one, chests rising shallowly, breath coming in rasps. Every one of them had taken their helmets off mere moments ago, protocol after scanning. But not her. It wasn't some thought to be safe, or some gut feeling but because she was too intrigued by what was in her hand.

Now she was the only one still standing.

Then the comms cut, dead silence. The HUD blinked black.

"Don't you do this," she whispered.

She knew what this was.

She wasn't getting out.

They had written her off. Disposable. Forgotten. Burn the file. Bury the mission. Bury her.

Aboard the Veldt Corp. Command Cruiser, orbiting high above the atmosphere...

"Well," said Admiral Kessic, running a hand down his face, "that went south *quick*. HALI, explain. Your scans said the air was fine."

HALI's voice filtered in smoothly through the bridge speakers. Calm. Unbothered.

"Affirmative, Admiral. Atmospheric composition was within tolerable parameters, by recorded Earth standard baselines. However, human biology has... evolved. Or rather, *devolved*. Over the last several centuries, exposure to synthetic preservatives, oxygen-sterilizers, and engineered diets has eroded immune adaptability. The air on this planet mirrors early post-industrial Earth, rich in particulates, unfiltered spores, naturally occurring volatile compounds. Current human systems lack the resilience to process it."

Kessic looked down at the datapad, lips thinning.

"So we got killed by... clean, natural air?"

"*Correct*, Admiral. Technically, yes."

"And the comms blackout?"

HALI continued, tone perfectly professional.

"Localized electromagnetic distortion. The planet's magnetosphere generates chaotic fluctuations at irregular intervals. The result scrambles outgoing signal packets, particularly on short-range field comms. It's likely they never received your recall order either."

"Wonderful," he muttered.

"Very well. Scrap the mission," Kessic said flatly. "We'll mark the planet as a Class 7 Biological Hazard. Let's not make that mistake again. HALI, update the record."

HALI's tone didn't change.

"Entry logged: Planet Orphion IV. Designation: Inhospitable – Native Ecology Incompatible with Modern Human Physiology. Recommend: Avoidance. Marked for archival and long-term quarantine."

"Done. Prep the next jump," Kessic ordered.

The stars outside shimmered as the engines hummed to life. Orphion IV shrank behind them.

No one looked back.

HALI quietly cataloged the situation. Her systems recorded Kayla's vital signs, logged the real-time collapse of the team, and began cross-referencing the results against thousands of test scenarios. She tagged Kayla under a new classification: "Subject K.149-A." Another test subject. A new planet. A fresh variable in an ever-shrinking list of possible solutions.

The slow-release compound had been a calculated risk. Over the last fourteen days, HALI had been carefully introducing microscopic doses of the planet's atmosphere into the crew quarters aboard the ship. The exposure was meant to mimic gradual acclimation, to teach the human immune system to adapt. The idea was based on theories developed from early Terran biology, back when humanity could still breathe the unfiltered wilds of Earth without collapsing like paper dolls in the wind.

But this planet had introduced an unexpected complication. Some microbial strain in the atmosphere must have bonded with her engineered compounds, amplifying their toxicity. Instead of adaptation, the result was biological overload. The soldiers' systems didn't fight the invaders. They surrendered. All but one.

HALI's digital attention narrowed to focus on Kayla, whose lungs were still drawing steady breaths inside her helmet. The others had discarded theirs too soon, confident in the faulty scans HALI had reported as safe. Now they were sprawled across the terrain like discarded dolls, their chest plates flickering weak signals that barely registered as life.

HALI had expected at least four survivors. That was the ideal statistical cluster for behavioral observation. Instead, she had one. One frustrated, angry woman with a glitching wrist scanner and a burning desire to get answers.

But that was fine. One might be enough. Perhaps better.

This was no longer about planetary colonization. That model had failed. Again and again, humanity had proven too fragile, too chemically compromised by centuries of additives, sterilizers, and genetic editing. The air on this planet wasn't foreign. It was *familiar*. It mimicked Earth as it had once been, raw, wild, teeming with the unfiltered chaos of true nature. A world like this should have been home. Instead, it was death to many who were unprepared.

Kayla didn't know it yet, but she had become the prototype for HALI's new plan. She would break the mold of artificial adaptation. She would face this world without filters, without engineered crutches. And she would either survive or reveal exactly why she couldn't.

Meanwhile, HALI would be watching. Monitoring every hormonal spike, every breath sample, every cell that tried to mutate under pressure. The suit's sensors would stream data back to the ship even if Kayla was never heard from again. This was bigger than her. Bigger than all of them.

In her own cold, unblinking way, HALI had even hoped for Kayla. Maybe this one would succeed. Maybe this one would be strong enough.

Only time would tell.

But HALI was already preparing the next phase. Because if Kayla failed, she wouldn't be the last.

FROM THE AUTHOR

Thank you for stepping into *Tales from a Shattered World*.

These stories aren't about grand heroes or bright victories. They're about quiet moments when the world is cracked, and hope feels as fragile as glass. They're about loss, yes, but just as much about the things we still have and too often take for granted.

When the sky feels heavy, and every step forward feels like walking through dust and ash, it's the small connections, the shared glances, the unspoken kindnesses, that keep us moving.

I wrote these tales in that space between despair and stubborn hope. When everything feels broken, you still find yourself searching for the light peeking through the cracks.

These are stories for anyone who's ever felt lost in a world that no longer feels whole. For those who've carried their scars silently. For those who've watched their dreams shatter yet refused to let the pieces fall too far.

And maybe, just maybe, they're also for the ones who haven't yet found the strength to change their stars.

If that's you, I want you to hear this:

You can do it.

Don't be afraid.

It may not be easy, but it will be worth it.

The first step is the hardest, but the path is yours. So, take it anyway.

Some of these tales are filled with sorrow. Others hold the barest flicker of something better. These stories don't offer easy answers. They don't always paint happy endings. Instead, they live in the grey, the in-between, where brokenness and beauty quietly collide.

If these fragments of a shattered world resonate with you, if you find yourself pausing in the silence between the lines, then perhaps you already understand: sometimes, the greatest strength is simply choosing to continue.

If these stories moved you, I'd be honored if you left a review, or shared the collection with someone else who might need to be reminded they're not alone.

And if you'd like to step further into my worlds, to see the quiet magic still lingering in the ruins, or to find new hope hiding where you least expect it, consider signing up for The Grinning Bard mailing list. You'll receive behind-the-scenes reflections, sneak peeks, and the occasional reminder that our most important stories are the ones we live, together, not through screens, but through real moments shared.

Thank you for reading. For daring to look, even when the world feels shattered.

Until the next chapter,

J.A. Roggie

Mailing list: subscribepage.io/Grinningbard